Top six reasons not to fall for the hunk next door:

1. You wake up every morning and see his handsome face—from the other side of the fence.

2. If you borrow another cup of sugar from him, you'll look suspicious.

3. His six-year-old son wants to spend Saturday night with you more than he does.

4. His kid brings out every maternal instinct you thought you never had.

5. *He* thinks you haven't got a maternal bone in your body.

6. Husbands don't grow on trees—least of all in your own backyard!

Dear Reader,

Personal ads? Full of those lonely hearts looking for love in all the wrong places? *Give me a break,* some of you are probably thinking.

Granted, in Dixie Browning's *Single Female (Reluctantly) Seeks...* JeanAnn Turner dates a few doozies until she figures out where to find Mr. Wonderful. But the title of Kasey Michaels's Yours Truly novel makes a very good point: *Husbands Don't Grow on Trees.*

That, I know. I also know that if you do nothing unexpected, nothing unexpected happens. So I checked out the personals for myself. Guess what? Some very wonderful, very eligible bachelors are behind those fifty little words. All kinds, from sexy daredevils to the boy next door.

Speaking of the boy next door, isn't he supposed to be the sweet, nice type? That's what Susannah Yardley thought before she met the sexy single father next door in Kasey Michaels's *Husbands Don't Grow on Trees.* Sweet, nice types don't make you want to borrow a cup of sugar at midnight.

Next month, look for Yours Truly titles by Laurie Paige and Hayley Gardner—two new novels about unexpectedly meeting, dating and marrying Mr. Right!

Yours Truly,

Melissa Senate
Editor

Please address questions and book requests to:
Silhouette Reader Service
U.S.: 3010 Walden Ave., P.O. Box 1325, Buffalo, NY 14269
Canadian: P.O. Box 609, Fort Erie, Ont. L2A 5X3

KASEY MICHAELS

Husbands Don't Grow on Trees

SILHOUETTE YOURS TRULY™

Published by Silhouette Books
America's Publisher of Contemporary Romance

SILHOUETTE BOOKS

ISBN 0-373-52008-5

HUSBANDS DON'T GROW ON TREES

Copyright © 1995 by Kasey Michaels

About the author

So, where does someone get the idea for a book about a love affair built around an eccentric old lady who takes up residence in a condemned tree house?

Beats me! And that's the fun of a Yours Truly. When I got the call from my editor, Anne Canadeo, asking me if I'd like to try my hand at a "funny, upbeat, hip" (yes, she said "hip") kind of book, I jumped at the chance. After publishing more than forty books, ranging from Regencies to historicals to contemporaries, even to nonfiction, the notion of just "letting it all hang out" in a book with basically no rules other than "just have fun!" was irresistible!

I hope you, dear reader, have as much fun reading *Husbands Don't Grow on Trees* as I did writing it. Just don't think I put myself in the book, as the character Aunt Bitzy, because I didn't—honest. I'm a sober, refined, utterly rational individual. Really. Hey! What are you laughing at?

To Joan Hohl, who is just as much "up a tree"
as I am, bless her, and to Gail Link,
who "gave" me Aunt Bitzy's tree house

1

It was Monday in Manhattan, and it was raining.

When combined with the fact that Cynthia Simons Thorogood had just canceled her appointment because she couldn't bear to come back from the Hamptons in "the midst of a deluge, my dear," for something as silly as a consultation with her interior decorator—it was enough to put a gal in the mood to chew nails.

Nothing so delicate on the old canines and incisors as finishing nails, either. Carpenter nails. Big ones. The kind that come in a paper sack.

Susannah Yardley, the "my dear" whom Mrs. Thorogood had just blown off for the third time in as many weeks, clutched a thick stack of mail she'd picked up in the lobby and shifted her overloaded cloth sack full of groceries closer against her left hip as she stepped out of the elevator and headed for her apartment.

Her blunt-cut, shoulder-length natural-blond hair still dripped rainwater since she had just walked a dozen blocks without once spying a vacant taxi. Her brand-new yet no-longer-white linen shoes made little squishing sounds as she stomped down the carpeted fifth-floor corridor, already embarked on a fishing expedition to hook her ring of keys somewhere deep within her cavernous purse.

Susannah Yardley was wet, she was tired, she was hungry, and she was miffed—which had been her mother's delicate way of describing her daughter's mood when, as an angelic-looking child, Susannah rolled on the floor in the midst of a temper tantrum, pounded her little fists on the carpet and screamed, "No! *No!*"

Susannah wanted a tepid shower, a hot meal, and a soft bed, in that order, and if anyone dared to so much as glance at her crookedly before she had at least two of those three things, she might make the banner headline for tomorrow's tabloids—Death by Designer, or some such drivel.

The long thin box of number-nine spaghetti hit the floor just as Susannah's fingers finally closed around her key ring, and she bit out a short oath as she worked both dead bolts, opened the door, and kicked the box inside.

"I buy the canned stuff myself," a perpetually cheery voice informed Susannah from just behind her. "I know it smells awful, but I like those cute animal shapes swimming in that ersatz marinara sauce. I give them all names—male names, names of creeps and losers I used to date—and then I chew them up. Chomp, chomp, chomp. *Jurassic Park*—the culinary soap-opera version. I think I'm slightly twisted, but, hey, who isn't these days? Want some help?''

Susannah's shoulders slumped just for a moment before she could paste a smile on her face and turn to see Brenda, her next-door neighbor, lurking in the hallway.

So much for best-laid plans. She couldn't say no to Brenda, who had been away on a job for the past two weeks or so. "Hi, Bren," she said dully, pushing an annoying, clinging strand of damp hair out of her eyes and motioning for her friend to precede her into the apartment. "So, when did you get back?"

"I landed in Newark around three, then had to fight traffic back to the city. Manhattan in the rain. Always such a joy. God forbid the agency could spring for a flight into JFK," Brenda told her as she picked up the box of pasta and headed for the small galley kitchen. Susannah had decorated her kitchen in green and white, using kelly green countertops, and ivy-patterned wallpaper to open up the space above ancient white cabinets.

"Here it is, the middle of June, and there I was for the last ten days, posing in woolens in Jamaica. Beige is the new color for winter, in case you're interested. Ecru, oatmeal—you name it, they have a dozen names for it—but it's still beige. It should suit you," Brenda continued, flinging herself onto a tall stool at the breakfast bar, "with all that blond hair *nobody* should be lucky enough to have been born with. You even look good sopping wet—not that the rain has done those shoes a world of good. Me, I wear wigs.''

Susannah plopped the cloth bag on the counter and began unloading groceries, longing for some aspirin, for Brenda's banter was adding insult to her already pounding headache. ''I noticed. I think I like you as a redhead, actually.''

''Well, enjoy it, because I'm back to my natural black tomorrow. We're doing a shoot of wedding gowns, and the manufacturer nixed any redheads. Too ho-ho-ho-ish for virginal brides, if you catch the drift. Oh, you bought one of those salads in a bag! Are they any good? Mom always said you shouldn't cut lettuce with a knife, and somehow I don't think that stuff was shredded by hand. I got some of your mail again. Hope it isn't important, because the postmark is darn near two weeks old. It looks like the same spidery handwriting of the other letters I've gotten that belonged to you. Must be a parochial-school graduate—they always have the neatest penmanship.''

''Do you ever breathe in between sentences, Brenda?'' Susannah teased, then paused in the act of tossing the bag of salad greens into the refrigerator in the hope the lettuce would crisp up a little, and forced her tired mind to wade through Brenda's jumbled speech and pick out the salient points.

''A letter? It must be from Aunt Bitzy. She always writes 5A instead of 5B, remember? I keep telling her not to, but she says I never had a B in my life, and she somehow equates academic grades with apartment numbers. In anyone else it would be strange, but with Aunt Bitzy, it all sort of makes a bizarre kind of sense. And you're half-right, Bren. Aunt Bitzy taught in a parochial grammar school—and penmanship was her forte. Do me a favor, will you, and open it? I want to get a pot of water on for the pasta, then jump into the shower. If you agree to rinse the lettuce in ice water, I'll even invite you for dinner.''

"Thanks, but no," Brenda said, already slitting the envelope with one of her long, bright-red faux nails. "Believe it or not, this girl's got herself a blind date— which just goes to show how much jet lag muddles the mind. Wow, what great handwriting. What do they call that stuff? Copperplate? I'm really impressed! It's only one page. Do you want me to read it to you?''

Susannah nodded, intent on employing all her remaining strength to twist open the jar of spaghetti sauce. It wasn't as if Aunt Bitzy was the risqué sort, peppering her letters with anything more racy than mention of the plot of one of the romance novels she borrowed by the bagful from the local library.

"'Dearest Cookie—' She's kidding, right? *Cookie?*''

Susannah leaned against the countertop, her green eyes soft, her smile dreamy. "It's a pet name from my childhood," she explained, suddenly not so tired or so out of sorts, even as the rain continued to beat loudly against the kitchen window. "I was a city kid, and every summer Mom and Dad sent me to Allentown to be with Aunt Bitzy and Uncle Frank. I *lived* for Aunt Bitzy's homemade chocolate-chip cookies.''

"Sounds nice," Brenda said, nodding and continuing to read. "'I think I should tell you that dearest Emily is in grave danger.' Wow! Now we're getting somewhere! She even underlined 'grave,''' Brenda exclaimed, hopping down from the stool. "'A stranger—' also underlined '—has come into the neighborhood and he has threatened to do away with Emily.'"

Brenda whistled. "'Do away' is printed in capital letters!'' She gave the paper another flourish and continued: "'As Emily was a particular favorite of both you and your dear uncle, I have taken it upon myself to save her from such a terrible and unwarranted fate—' All right, Aunt Bitzy! Go for it!''

"Give me that!" Susannah demanded, ripping the letter from her friend's hands, mumbling her way through the part Brenda had already read before quickly quoting aloud: "'Please do not concern yourself in the matter, for I have thought the thing out rationally and know just what must be done. I plan to stay with Emily until this evil man, this vile, encroaching predator, learns the folly of his destructive plan. So, dear Cookie, do not worry if you do not hear from me for a time, as Emily has no telephone. With love, Aunt Bitzy.' Oh, my *God!*''

Clutching the letter to her chest, Susannah slowly settled herself cross-legged on the cool tile floor, shaking her head as she tried to compose herself. "I don't believe it. No, that's a lie. Face it, *Cookie*. You do believe it. After all, it's Aunt Bitzy. Dad always told us to remember that Bitzy rhymes with 'ditzy.'"

"Well, this isn't exactly being productive, is it? Stop talking to yourself," Brenda ordered, stepping over Susannah as she crossed to the stove to turn down the heat under the now boiling water. "You can't let an old lady try to stop a killer. You know what you oughta do? I'll tell you what you oughta do. You oughta to get up, shake yourself off, and call the police in this burg—this Allentown. Omigod! Unless— Jeez. This letter is nearly two weeks old! It could already be too late. For crying out loud. Susannah! Would you *please* get up from the floor and call the police?"

"Nobody's killing anybody, Bren," Susannah told Brenda as she wearily got to her feet, wondering idly if one of the rain clouds had followed her inside, for she was getting the strange feeling that she had been struggling against some sort of award-winning run of bad luck all day.

"Oh, yeah?" Brenda countered, grabbing the letter and waving it beneath Susannah's chin. "What about Emily? It sure sounds like somebody is trying to kill her."

"I agree, Bren, it sure sounds like it," Susannah said, summoning a small smile as she pushed a hand through her hair. "Except for one thing. Emily, you see, is a *tree!*"

2

➤ ◄━

She could have just phoned her parents, Susannah knew, and let her capable father handle things from his end. Aunt Bitzy was his sister-in-law, after all.

But Florida was such a long way away, and she was so close, and—thanks to Cynthia Simons Thorogood—with nothing to keep her in Manhattan during the first heat wave of the summer, the least she could do was to go rescue the poor man who had innocently run afoul of her lovable but eccentric aunt.

At least that's what Susannah told herself as she steered the rental car down the highway toward Pennsylvania, and Allentown, and Belinda "Bitzy" Yardley.

Besides, it was always cooler in Aunt Bitzy's shady backyard swing than it could ever be on the white-hot concrete pavements of Manhattan. She could sit on the brick patio with her aunt, using one bare big toe to propel the swing, sipping fresh home-squeezed lemonade, counting the stars through the trees, talking about those long-ago summers when she had liked being called "Cookie"....

It would be lovely. Simply lovely.

"If only I can get good old Aunt Bitzy out of that damned tree!" she said aloud as she put the pedal to the floor in order to pass a huge tractor-trailer lumbering slowly up the last good hill before the cut-off to Allentown.

She pulled off Route 22 at the first exit showing a Golden Arches sign and sat on a concrete bench sipping a cold soda as she recalled her summers with Aunt Bitzy and Uncle Frank.

They had been wonderful summers, full of lazy days and quiet nights so unlike the hustle and bustle of New York. She had made new friends, of course, and visited the local swimming pools, but for the most part she had reveled in the attention of her aunt and uncle, two of the most uniquely individual people she had ever known.

Childless themselves, they had lavished all their love on Susannah, even going so far as to build her a tree house in the old elm on the adjoining, vacant property.

Emily.

Aunt Bitzy had given the tree that name, in the same lovable but faintly eccentric way she christened most everything for which she felt affection. Her old sedan was Rachel, the backyard swing was Robert, the antique gas stove in the kitchen was Daisy Sue—and the elm tree was Emily.

This ritual naming of inanimate objects had made perfect sense to a nine-year-old, and it still did, which just proved to Susannah that she was badly in need of a vacation. Not that this trip to Allentown looked to be anything approaching restful.

Not with Aunt Bitzy living in the old tree house, daring her new, nameless neighbor to cut Emily down in the name of progress or for whatever reason the man had for taking an ax to an old Yardley family member.

Unless, she thought as she tossed the paper cup into a trash container, Aunt Bitzy had already fallen out of the tree and was even now lying in some hospital, her hip broken. Or, perhaps even scarier, if she hadn't been arrested for trespassing and thrown into the local slammer, where she was probably busy giving names to her cot and commode.

Susannah got back into the rental car and headed toward the rambling house on Highland Avenue—or toward "Thomas," as Aunt Bitzy referred to the two-story brick dwelling.

She pulled into the driveway behind a second-generation ancient Buick ten minutes later and stepped from the car, listening to the suburban silence that was broken only by birdsong and the rustle of a cooling breeze high in the tall oak trees.

All the oaks were over one hundred years old, which had made them unsuitable for a tree house, Susannah remembered. Uncle Frank hadn't worried about building a tree house in Emily because no one had ever lived on the sloping acre of open land behind Thomas and he'd doubted anyone ever would.

It had all seemed so simple, so reasonable, at the time.

Leaving her few pieces of luggage in the back seat, Susannah skirted around Thomas—really! she should stop thinking of the house as a person!—and headed for the backyard, hoping against hope that the tree house was unoccupied.

But it wasn't to be.

She had taken no more than three steps past Robert when she heard the sound of raised voices, the loudest being that of Aunt Bitzy as she primly recited from Joyce Kilmer's "Trees": "'I think that I shall never see/A poem lovely as a tree—' No, don't speak. There's more. Give me a moment, please, and I shall recall it."

Susannah peered through the oaks to see the outline of the old elm, and a small white-haired lady perched halfway up it on the front porch of the large, weather-stained tree house.

"Oh, good grief!" Susannah exclaimed, breaking into a run.

Jake Longstreet saw the blonde out of the corner of his eye and spared a moment to admire her long, bare legs as she approached, then turned once more to listen to Belinda Yardley. The woman was a real character, and he liked her very much.

Not that he was finding the petite, apple-cheeked, gray-haired lady very entertaining at the moment. Not when she was playing Queen of the Tree House, re-galing the local media with her earnest recitations.

He didn't know how it had happened but, wanting only to cut down a dying, potentially dangerous tree, he had somehow been cast in the role of Allentown's resident "dastardly villain."

And, after two weeks of this wacky stuff, it was be-ginning to get pretty tiresome!

"Ah, yes, I have it now. I'll begin again from the beginning, shall I?" Mrs. Yardley was saying as Jake looked toward the condemned tree, and the woman who had set up camp in its branches and, seemingly, in his life. "It goes just so— 'I think that I shall never see—'"

"'A billboard lovely as a tree./Indeed, unless the billboards fall/I'll never see a tree at all.'"

Mrs. Yardley frowned, her look of confused con-sternation causing Jake's lips to twitch in amusement at the newly arrived blonde's recitation of Ogden Nash's comic ditty. "No, no. That's not it. Kilmer mentioned nothing of billboards, although you have put forth a reasonable argument for trees. However, I'm quite convinced that—*Cookie!*"

Cookie? Jake's left eyebrow rose a fraction as he attempted to apply the name to the blonde, and failed miserably. She reminded him more of a long-stemmed glass of the finest Chardonnay.

Cool, yet sparkling; glowing, sleek, and sophisti-cated. Her sleeveless blouse was of soft ivory silk, her delightfully brief shorts a splash of emerald green linen that matched her eyes, her skin slightly golden—and eminently untouchable. *Cookie?* Hardly. And yet—

"Yes, Aunt Bitzy, it's Cookie," the blonde said soothingly as the trio of reporters standing around the base of the elm tree stood back and allowed her to approach. "You look wonderful, although I shudder to think how you got that rocking chair up there. How's Emily?"

Oh, great, Jake thought ruefully, stuffing his hands in his slacks pockets. *Just what this farce needs—another nut case. Emily. Even Alex has begun calling the damned tree by name, all the time glaring at me as if I'm some kind of bloodthirsty ax murderer, a serial killer with a thing for elm trees and sweet old ladies.*

"She's fine, for now," Mrs. Yardley answered, giving the large branch beside her a loving pat. "But first things first, Cookie. Remember your manners. Gentlemen, I'd like to introduce you to my niece, Susannah Yardley. She lives in Manhattan now, but this is really her tree house. Let's see—"

She squinted as she looked down from her perch, then continued, "Cookie, the gentleman to your left is David Serfass, who has come all the way from the Easton newspaper, and to your right are Stephen Wadlow, a columnist for our local newspaper, and his photographer, Edward Hunsberger. I taught Edward in the third grade, didn't I, Edward? He was a good student, although he did bite his nails." She smiled. "But you don't do that anymore now that you're all grown up, do you, Edward?"

The photographer hid his camera, and his hands, behind his back. "No, ma'am, Mrs. Yardley," he said, flushing to the roots of his receding hairline.

"That's nice, Edward," Mrs. Yardley commended him, then looked past the fibbing nail biter, her faded blue eyes clouding with what looked to be genuine pain and compassion. "Lastly, Cookie, I would be remiss if I did not introduce my new neighbor—"

"Jake Longstreet, Miss Yardley," Jake interrupted quickly, extending a hand to her before her aunt could introduce him as she had to the press, calling him "that unfortunate gentleman who is out to murder Emily."

Susannah Yardley looked to her aunt, and then at Jake's outstretched hand, which she then pointedly ignored. "Jake Longstreet? Ah, yes, you would be the 'vile, encroaching predator' of Aunt Bitzy's letter. You must be proud of yourself, Mr. Longstreet," she said so frostily that he felt a sudden chill descend over the sweltering afternoon. "We could have a nice little chat about your reasons for alarming my aunt, but I do believe you might be trespassing."

Jake dropped his hand as Edward Hunsberger lifted the camera to snap a picture of the rebuff and gritted out quietly, "Don't do it, nail biter, or I'll tell on you, and you'll have to stay after school. I'll bet you were great at clapping erasers, weren't you, *Edward?*"

Susannah's soft laughter bubbled up refreshingly, like cool water trickling over pebbles in a country stream, and Jake shot her a look, once more liking what he saw.

All right, so she was a flake, like the aunt. But he liked the aunt. He could like the niece. Hell, he could bed the niece—if he was that kind of guy. Which he wasn't. At least he'd like to think he wasn't; not anymore. Not since Jennifer. And definitely not since Alex.

"Aunt Bitzy didn't make anyone clap erasers, Mr. Longstreet," Susannah told him now, evidently oblivious to any notion that he, Jake, had just fought a small battle with his better self and was even now wishing that he'd lost. "She assigned essays on the evils of whatever we had done wrong. Didn't she, Mr. Hunsberger? I remember one I did for coming home after dark when I'd been told time and time again to be in the backyard, sitting quietly on Robert, five minutes before the streetlights went on."

"Sitting? On Robert? Now, there's a picture." *Good old conscience*, Jake congratulated his better self. *Keep me on the straight and narrow. Last thing I need at the moment is a ding-a-ling, no matter how beautiful she is.*

"Robert is the name Aunt Bitzy gave to the old swing on the back porch," Susannah informed him icily—her mood changing the weather for Jake yet again—then turned to look up at her aunt. "Aunt Bitzy?" she called out. "This is all quite lovely, and I'm sure I should be serving tea or something but— why are all these men here?"

Mrs. Yardley sighed, rolling her eyes. "I would have thought it was obvious, Cookie," she said, beginning to fan herself with a small bouquet of elm leaves. "They're here to learn all about Emily's sad plight."

She waggled the fan in Susannah's direction. "I may be an old lady, Cookie, but I do know the power of the press. Mightier than the sword, dear child, mightier than the sword—or the ax! Emily and I have already been featured on the local nightly television news, you know. Lovely commentator, although a trifle nasal. Hay fever, no doubt."

Aunt Bitzy frowned, then continued, "Or a deviated septum. Uncle Frank had a deviated septum, if you'll recall, and snored most prodigiously all through rose and ragweed seasons."

Jake smiled with personal satisfaction as Susannah Yardley sighed and the reporters grinned and scribbled in their notebooks, taking down every word the old woman said. Maybe this wasn't so bad after all. The more Belinda Yardley opened her mouth, the more she ran the chance of making a local joke of herself—*and* her blasted "cause."

If I can just hold out, Jake thought smugly, *and hold on to my temper, Fred might be able to knock down the tree within the week—*

The two reporters tucked their notebooks into their hip pockets and nodded to Jake as they drifted away together, Stephen Wadlow calling over his shoulder, "One more picture of the gorgeous niece, Eddie. I've got a good column here. If we're lucky, and the old girl doesn't fall out of the tree, we can milk the human-interest angle on this baby for another month!''

Then again, Jake told himself, shrugging wryly as he took another look at Susannah Yardley's long legs as she climbed the curving steps up to the tree house, *maybe a month wasn't long enough....*

Jake the Elm Tree Killer was gorgeous.

Aunt Bitzy had failed to mention that in her letter, but there was no denying the obvious.

The man was more than gorgeous—he was knee-meltingly gorgeous. Hair like night. Blue eyes. Eyebrows like raven's wings—and as expressive as all hell.

Bedroom eyes. That's what Brenda would call them. The nose? Thin. Straight. Forgettable, but then Susannah had never considered herself to be a nose person. Ah, but the planes of those high-boned cheeks, and that slashing, sarcastic invitation of a mouth—those interested her very much!

He looked like the actor, Pierce Brosnan, she decided, but with none of Brosnan's British reserve.

He wore well-cut dark slacks with front pleats, like Brosnan, and his shirt was Brosnan crisp white against his tan.

But he was a few inches taller than the movie star, and broader in the shoulders, although his hips were dangerously, provocatively narrow above long legs.

All in all, a man to die for—to use another "Brenda-ism."

Not that I'm interested, Susannah reminded herself as she kissed her aunt's papery, powder-sweet cheek, then sat down cross-legged on the narrow front porch of the tree house, looking out over the Yardley backyard, deliberately keeping her glancing eyes at least seven feet above the ground.

The tree house was reached via a trunk-hugging, winding set of wooden stairs, complete with handrail, as Uncle Frank had been a stickler for safety. The gray, weathered boards of the small front porch matched the gray, weathered boards of the octagonal-shaped tree house, built to fit neatly inside the wide, up-turned-palm, spread-fingers cradle of branches. The tree house had a sloping roof, one door, and six glass-paned windows.

A veritable engineering feat, as a matter of fact.

And the repository of a million wonderful childhood memories.

"A real hunk, isn't he?" Aunt Bitzy trilled at last, giving Susannah a nudge with one slippered foot as she broke into her niece's reverie.

"Aunt Bitzy!" Susannah exclaimed, shaking her head. "Shame on you."

"Nonsense, Cookie. I'm old, not dead. He reminds me of Slade Ramsey, the hero in *Destiny's Sweet Promise,* the latest book from Araminta Raven—my favorite author, if you'll recall. Slade was an Alpha hero, too, with a dangerous dark side. Men are so exciting when they have dark sides, don't you think, Cookie?"

Susannah kept a straight face, but only with difficulty. Old-fashioned, otherworldly, Aunt Bitzy had one innocent vice—her beloved romance novels. "Did Uncle Frank have a dark side, Aunt Bitzy?" she asked, once more painfully aware that Jake Longstreet remained standing near the base of the elm tree, waiting . . . for what, she didn't know.

It was a shame Emily wasn't a palm tree, so that she could bomb him with coconuts.

"Oh, dear me, yes, Cookie," Aunt Bitzy said, patting the gray bun at the top of her head. "He may not have been dark, or brooding, but he had a deeply passionate nature. Why, I remember the time—we were attending a teachers' convention in Pittsburgh—well, he saw this *man,* this mathematics instructor from Reading, *looking* at me over the fruit cup at the banquet."

"Ogled you over the pineapple chunks, huh?" Susannah teased. "Sounds pretty risqué to me."

"Yes, indeed, Cookie. Frank was *incensed,* for he always said mathematics instructors are entirely too interested in figures! He all but *dashed* me from the banquet hall and into the first available elevator. And then, even as the car was climbing to the twentieth floor—"

Susannah leaned forward eagerly. "Yes? And then?"

Aunt Bitzy patted her bun again, her apple-round cheeks coloring a becoming pink, her faded blue eyes dancing with secret memories. "Never mind, Cookie. After all, you are an unmarried woman."

"Miss Yardley?"

Susannah flinched at the sound of Jake Longstreet's black velvet voice, then reluctantly leaned forward, looking down at the man with, hopefully, a face drenched in disdain. "You're still here, Mr. Longstreet? Isn't it time you crawled back under your rock? Or do you get your kicks harassing harmless old women?"

"Cookie, be polite," Aunt Bitzy whispered. "Firm, but polite."

"I'll be slithering away in a minute or two, Miss Yardley," Jake called up to her, seemingly undaunted by her try at sarcasm, "but first I'd like to remind you that now, as chance would have it, *you* are trespassing. Emily—that is, this elm tree—is on *my* property."

Susannah looked at Aunt Bitzy. "He had it surveyed, didn't he? Oh, never mind. Of course he had it surveyed. He's just the sort to want to know just what he owns, down to the last square inch."

She leaned forward a little farther, until she was able to see the dark glints of amusement in the man's eyes. Amusement gained at her expense, she was sure.

Pierce Brosnan would never laugh at a lady. He was too British, too mannerly. But not Jake Longstreet. He wouldn't only laugh at a lady, he'd evict one from her beloved tree house.

It was strange. She had come here hoping to help the man out of what had to be an embarrassing situation. And yet it had taken only a single look, a single word from his intriguing lips, to change her mind, so that she now saw him as the enemy.

All he needed was a black cape he could flourish and a long, thin mustache he could twirl as he laughed maniacally while he evicted the sweet little old lady and her beautiful young niece from their beloved family home, casting them out into the cold, cruel world with only the clothes on their backs...unless the beautiful young niece agreed to—

Would you cut it out! Susannah ordered her wandering mind.

Maybe, she decided, she was dehydrated from the heat of the two-hour drive. The rental car's air conditioner hadn't worked well, and she had only ordered a small soda at the fast-food restaurant.

But, no. That wasn't it. She simply had met Jake Longstreet and immediately tensed up, put herself on guard. As if he were not only a threat to Emily, but a more personal threat, as well. Which was silly. Completely, perfectly silly!

"Can we talk?" Susannah asked, hating herself for giving an inch. However, as she hadn't as yet figured out how her aunt had been able to live comfortably in the old tree house—and was equally sure she didn't want to learn how—she saw only one option open to her: that of trying to reason with the infuriating Jake Longstreet.

He lifted his left forearm, pushing back his shirt-sleeve to glance at the sleek gold watch that spanned his wrist. *Probably a counterfeit, like those rip-offs you can pick up in Times Square for twenty bucks,* Susannah thought nastily, knowing she was wrong. There was nothing remotely counterfeit about this man. If anything, he was *too* real for her peace of mind.

"It's four o'clock, nearly time for Alex—that's my son, you understand—to take up his guard duties with Mrs. Yardley. If we hurry, we can grab a cup of coffee at a restaurant about a mile from here, and be back before dinnertime. Is that all right with you, Mrs. Yardley?"

His son? Susannah sighed, covering her disappointed reaction with a quick cough as she checked out his left, ring-free hand.

"Mr. Longstreet's a widower, Cookie," Aunt Bitzy whispered confidingly, her smile heavy with meaning.

All right, so he was a widower, not that Susannah cared if he was married. Or divorced. Or even living in sin. He was single, and that was bad enough. *And I'll bet he has a freezer full of tuna-noodle casseroles brought to him by all the local, single women who are loony enough to think Jake Longstreet's some kind of great catch.*

Not that she, Susannah Who-would-never-be-so-obvious Yardley, would ever stoop so low.

"Mrs. Yardley?" Jake prompted when the woman didn't answer. Aunt Bitzy sat silently, her invisible "thinking cap," as she'd explained it once to a much younger Susannah, obviously in place.

At last Aunt Bitzy nodded, saying, "I think I have a better idea. Alex will be fine with me, Mr. Longstreet, as always. We can share soup and sandwiches for a light dinner, then sit with Robert and talk over our day, while you and Cookie can dine at the restaurant. She has skipped lunch, if I know my Cookie, as she eats like a bird when she's upset. Until tomorrow morning at seven?"

"I believe birds eat something in the way of twice their own weight every day, but I think my budget can handle it. Come along, Miss Yardley, as I'm getting a stiff neck looking up at you. Until tomorrow morning, Mrs. Yardley. Have a good evening," Jake said as Susannah, who was thoroughly confused—not to mention downright *maddened*—by this conversation, looked to her aunt for rescue.

"Aunt Bitzy?" she questioned the older woman under her breath. "Aren't you afraid he'll have Emily cut down while you're cooking dinner?"

"No, no, my dear," Aunt Bitzy answered, reaching out to pat Susannah's cheek. "We have arrived at a mutually pleasing understanding, Mr. Longstreet and I. If he gives me the hours between five in the afternoon and seven in the morning to refresh myself in my own house, and if I spend the hours between seven and five in the tree house, my crusade can continue."

"Well, I guess that's sensible, in some bizarre, wacko sort of way," Susannah mumbled, wondering if she should be looking around for the rabbit hole she had toppled down the moment her sandaled feet hit the Yardley driveway.

"But he is not without an ulterior motive, of course," Aunt Bitzy continued matter-of-factly. "He's hoping the July heat will be my downfall, and that I'll give in eventually and allow Fred Gibbons to chop Emily down. Isn't that right, Mr. Longstreet?" she called out as Susannah shook her head and then slowly, reluctantly, quit the tree house, hoping a return to solid ground might clear her mind.

"Partly, Mrs. Yardley," Jake answered, offering his arm to Susannah—a polite gesture she refused to either acknowledge or accept. They reached the brick path Uncle Frank had laid thirty years previously. "To be perfectly honest, Miss Yardley, my life wasn't easy until I agreed to this arrangement. Alex was beginning to look at me as if I was a first-class bas—"

"We quite understand, Mr. Longstreet," Aunt Bitzy interrupted sternly from her perch in the elm tree, employing her best, carrying, schoolteacher tones.

"Sorry," Jake said, looking suitably sheepish. There wasn't a man born who could hold up under one of Aunt Bitzy's loving rebukes.

"Indeed," Aunt Bitzy continued, her tone milder, but still definitely fixed in her schoolteacher mode. There was no need to expound, now was there? And certainly no need for vulgar profanities. "Now, you two just run along while I locate my copy of *Tom Sawyer*. I think I hear Alex's camp bus pulling up now, and if I know that boy, he'll want me to read him another chapter.''

Fighting the feeling that she'd just been handed over to the Romans for a stint in the Colosseum, Susannah protested, ''This is ridiculous! I can't go to dinner in shorts, Aunt Bitzy. I'll have to shower, and change, and—no. It's just too much trouble. I'll just unpack and then have soup and sandwiches, too.''

She looked at Jake, immediately hating him for smiling at her just as if he knew she was deliberately trying to avoid being alone with him. ''Maybe some other time?''

''Chicken, Miss Yardley?'' he challenged quietly, that miserably attractive, mocking left eyebrow climbing toward the dark sweep of hair that fell forward onto his smooth brow.

''That's *Ms.* Yardley,'' Susannah shot back, tilting her chin in a defensive manner. ''And meet me out front in twenty minutes!''

With that said, she wheeled about and headed for her car to get her luggage, cursing herself every step of the way for reacting like some laboratory rat—responding predictably to a tired childhood dare, and ending by doing precisely what she hadn't intended to do at all.

3

→ ←

Susannah Yardley had looked great in shorts, but she looked even better in a dress. Sleeker. Crazily, she looked even longer-limbed above two-inch heels that accented her slim, pretty ankles.

She had a long sweep of a back, a pleasurably ample portion of which was exposed by the sleeveless sundress of pale green cotton, and her narrow waist all but cried out to be spanned by his long-fingered hands.

And any jury of her peers would probably declare her "not guilty" for murdering him if he even tried to touch her.

Jake wondered why Susannah Yardley had met him and taken such an instant dislike to him, but he didn't wonder about it long, for he'd never had much trouble attracting women.

This one might just take a little longer to convince, that was all.

Not that he was interested in either the chase or the capture, he reminded himself while he smiled a greeting as Susannah walked down the length of the driveway and gracefully entered the low-slung sports car without thanking him for holding open the passenger door for her.

Jake shut the door firmly, then tapped the roof of the midnight blue sports car with one dismissive hand before jogging around to the driver's side and sliding his long legs under the dash.

"Nice dress," he said as he turned the key, setting the powerful engine into its instant, purring rumble.

"Thank you. I see you've got New York plates on this juvenile, masculine status symbol, Mr. Longstreet," Susannah replied, keeping her chin high and her gaze aimed at the windshield as he backed the car into the driveway and turned around.

All right, lady, Jake decided, hiding a smile. *If you want to play, we'll play.*

"Yes, even us sophisticated, New York City-type Alpha males—your aunt's description, and one I sure as hell don't understand—enjoy our phallic toys. That is what you liberated female types call them, isn't it? I've seen the commercials, you understand—the ones where a group of very modern women stand around judging men by their cars."

Her beautifully sculpted chin never budged. "We modern, liberated female types are not the *ones* who dubbed cars like this one 'hot *rods.*'"

Jake threw back his head and laughed. "I have to admit it, Susannah. I never really considered the subject before now. I hereby apologize, and will trade in the sports car tomorrow for something politically correct. How about a minivan?''

Susannah turned and smiled at him. ''Which one, Jake?'' she asked, also addressing him on a first-name basis. ''The manufacturers have come up with equally amusing names for those, too. Will you go for the desert-sheik motif, or the star-wars approach to masculine adventure?''

''I give up, and plead guilty for the entire male population,'' Jake answered, shaking his head as he eased into the traffic on Cedar Crest Boulevard.

''If you'll take it on a one-way trip back to Manhattan, I don't care if you drive a dump truck,'' Susannah quipped, facing front once more, the lift of her chin telling him she was still hating him—a lot— even before she asked tightly, ''How dare you persecute an old woman?''

''Well, you see, I was getting bored pulling wings off butterflies,'' he supplied angrily, ''and then— presto!—there she was, perched in that damned tree, and I thought, hey, Jake, why not? She's old, she's frail, she's ripe for the plucking. Why not see if you can do everything you can to make her life miserable? It wasn't much of a challenge, you understand, what with her being sixty-something if she's a day, and stuck in a tree with only a thermos of tea, and a couple of dull knitting needles as weapons, but what the hell—''

''All right, all right,'' Susannah interrupted just as testily. ''I believe I get the point. Aunt Bitzy started this. But you're the one who wants to chop down Emily. Can't you see that she's only trying to protect her memories? Do you need the tree house gone that badly?''

Jake steered the car into the parking lot of the Reflections of Life restaurant, cutting the engine before answering. "I like the tree," he said simply, succinctly, deliberately using words with the fewest syllables. "Alex likes the tree. All God's children are crazy about the damned tree."

"So? What's the problem? If you like the tree, then why not— "

"It's dying, Susannah, *that's* the problem. It's got deep frost cracks all over it from that lousy winter of two years ago. There were one hundred inches of snow in Allentown that winter, if you didn't know, and more ice storms than anyone can remember. The worst winter in recent memory, or so the locals tell me. Every nail your uncle drove into that tree is now a festering wound, and this past winter didn't help."

"I—I didn't know," Susannah said, biting her bottom lip. "Can't she be saved?"

"Maybe, if she was younger, stronger—and if nobody had built a tree house in her." He opened the driver's-side door, then looked back at Susannah. "Would you listen to me? I sound like I'm talking about a person, instead of a stupid tree! Life was easier in Manhattan. Muggers. Carjackers. Cockroaches. And none of them had names!"

When he came around the car to open Susannah's door he took a deep breath and continued: "It's a tree, Susannah, no matter how much your aunt loves it. A tree. And I can't take the chance that it won't become a death trap. It isn't yet—or at least Fred says it isn't. But in six months? After another hard winter? Your aunt's beloved Emily is nothing more than a dangerous, attractive nuisance, and I'll be damned if I'll take the chance that my son is in the tree when it finally splits and the tree house comes tumbling down."

This time Susannah did thank him for opening the door, and even took his offered hand as he assisted her out of the car. "Have you said all this to Aunt Bitzy?" she asked as they headed into the restaurant.

He waited until they had been seated at a window overlooking the greenery of Trexler Park before answering. "I explained everything to your aunt. Fred explained everything to your aunt. But Fred was not one of your aunt's best students. Something about a geography assignment and how he always took the easiest way out of a problem—believe me, don't ask!—and she decided upon a second opinion. The second opinion was that some of the cracks may close again over the summer and, if we don't have another really bad winter, the tree might eventually recover. Your aunt is betting on a decade of mild winters."

"Is she right?"

Jake ordered a Manhattan and Susannah asked for a glass of white wine. Once the waitress left, he explained, "I don't have any degrees in tree surgery or whatever, but Fred said that once a frost crack occurs, the tree is predisposed to cracking again from winter to winter, even if some of the cracks close in the summer. I made a few calls to other tree nurseries, and they confirmed Fred's diagnosis. It has been nearly two years, and the worst of the cracks are still there.''

"That's not good," Susannah said, wincing.

"No, it's not. And, depending on the location of the cracks, and their length, a structural weakness could develop, a weakness bad enough to require steel support cables and rods.''

Susannah shrugged. "So? Put in cables and rods."

"We could, if it weren't for the tree house. Emily already has more nail holes in her than a slice of good Swiss cheese. In her case, the cure would probably kill her. The tree has to come down, Susannah, that's the bottom line. I won't put my son's safety in jeopardy.''

Susannah thanked the waitress for the wine before ordering a chef's salad without even looking at the menu. Jake, also not looking at the menu, ordered a New York strip steak for himself, then winked at the waitress while canceling the chef's salad and ordering a petite filet mignon for Susannah—medium rare, just the way he liked it.

"You're a bit of a minor despot, aren't you, Mr. Longstreet? A chef's salad would have been more than enough for me, no matter what Aunt Bitzy says. Besides, I barely ever eat red meat,'' she protested as the waitress moved off toward the kitchen.

"So make an exception," Jake said, lifting the Manhattan to his lips. "I figured you needed something bloody to chew on so you wouldn't be tempted to take a bite out of me. You are still seeing me as the bad guy, aren't you? Even when I'm being sane, and eminently rational?"

Susannah fiddled with her fork for a moment, then, seemingly realizing that she was fidgeting, folded her hands together on the edge of the table. "Frankly, Jake, I don't know what to think. I mean, on the one hand, there is the matter of safety to consider. But, on the other hand, Fred could be wrong, and Emily might heal. Couldn't you simply order your son away from the tree house, and then wait to see what happens this winter?"

Jake smiled. "You were never nine, Susannah? Telling Alex to stay away is like an invitation to have him take up permanent residence in the tree house. I had enough trouble keeping him away from the construction site until all the interior walls and staircases were in."

"I thought I saw the roofline of a new house beyond the trees," Susannah said, looking up at him again, so that he was once more struck by her cool, sea green eyes. "It appears to be rather large for two people."

"Six bedrooms," Jake told her, trying to keep the pride from his voice. "Even with my main offices in Manhattan, I still needed a place large enough to work in, and roomy enough for some of my staff or clients to stay over if the situation warrants."

"I don't understand. You work in Manhattan—and at home?"

Now Jake was surprised, and mentally kicked himself for thinking Susannah would have heard his name and instantly recognized it. Maybe being lawyer to the stars wasn't enough to put his name on quite everyone's lips. Lord knew, it hadn't done much to impress Alex, his own son.

"I'm an attorney, Susannah, with my practice limited to the entertainment industry, mostly Broadway," he told her as the waitress placed salads in front of them.

He imagined he could see a light bulb going on over Susannah's blond head as she pointed her fork at him—a cherry tomato impaled on its tines. "*Remembering Mavis!* I saw that last fall! I stick with the musicals—*Les Misérables, Phantom of the Opera*—so of course I saw that one, too. *You're* the guy who made them use that marvelous English singer when they didn't want to, aren't you? Your name is always in the papers! Good Lord, I'm having dinner with a celebrity. Brenda will swoon when I tell her."

And then she frowned, and Jake's heart skipped a beat.

She remembers. Damn it—she remembers Jennifer!

"Wait a minute. This doesn't make sense. What's a big-time entertainment lawyer doing in Allentown?"

She doesn't remember. Maybe I'm overly impressed with my single fling with notoriety—and no one remembers.

"Raising a son on my own," Jake answered in hopefully well-disguised relief as Susannah popped the cherry tomato into her mouth. He tried not to concentrate on the way her pink-tinted lips closed around the fruit, or the vegetable, or whatever tomatoes were supposed to be. Right now, the only way he could describe the thing was *lucky*.

"The city is no place for a kid," he went on quickly. "And when a friend in publishing told me about Allentown, and how convenient it is to New York, I thought I'd give it a look. It turned out to be perfect. I plan to either drive into the city when I have to, or take the shuttle from the airport."

"But you're not living in Allentown now. You can't be, if your house isn't done."

"I got lucky. We're leasing the house next door to my property. The owners are in California, visiting their first grandchild until September, and jumped at the chance to pick up some rent money. I wanted to keep a close eye on the construction, for one thing, and now I have to stay close—thanks to your Aunt Bitzy. She's got a real local media circus going on, you know, complete with nasal reporters."

"Poor Jake," Susannah commiserated, her green eyes sparkling with mischief as she dabbed at her lips with the snow-white linen napkin. "Madonna must have taken a few days off, and my aunt is the biggest thing to happen in a slow news week. Well, sorry, Jake, but it's settled now. Aunt Bitzy has to stay in the tree house, at least a little while longer. We can't disappoint all those inquiring minds that think they have a right to know everything. Ah! Here come the steaks. Suddenly I'm ravenous!''

Susannah sat on the backyard swing, using the bare toe of one foot to idly push the ancient metal contraption back and forth as she rested her head against a pillow and gazed up at the rapidly darkening sky.

"Did he kiss you good-night?"

Patting the cushion beside her, inviting her aunt to sit down, Susannah sighed and said, "You know, we've got to find you another hobby, Aunt Bitzy. These romance novels are beginning to corrupt your schoolteacher morals."

"Romance, dear Cookie, is the *most* moral thing in this universe," her aunt corrected, offering Susannah a plate of her locally famous, homemade chocolate-chip cookies. "Your uncle Frank considered it to be our good Lord's finest creation. Now, please answer the question. Did Jake Longstreet kiss you good-night?"

"No, Aunt Bitzy, he most certainly did not," Susannah answered sternly as she visually examined the cookies, then picked up the one with the most chocolate chips. "And if he had tried it—tried anything at all—I would have clobbered him. We had a reasonably pleasant dinner, and then he drove me straight home. Does that answer your question?"

"It tells me that you still haven't recovered from that unfortunate interlude with that Marvin person."

"His name was Matthew, it all was over two years ago, and I have, too, recovered," Susannah said around a mouthful of cookie, pleased to realize that she was telling the truth. "I'm only thankful I found out in time that his idea of a full life was a big house, two luxury cars, a trophy wife to hang on his arm at cocktail parties—and no encumbering children. As if I could be happy without at least the prospect of having kids one day."

Aunt Bitzy nodded her agreement. "A man who doesn't love children is a sorry specimen, indeed. I wish your uncle Frank and I could have had a dozen, Cookie, but if it wasn't to be, at least we still had the love."

"Which you showered so freely on me," Susannah said, reaching over to give her aunt a hug, feeling a tug at her heart when she sniffed a nostalgic hint of lavender in the woman's hair. "If I haven't thanked you for that, Aunt Bitzy, please let me tell you now that you made my childhood a joy. A pure joy!"

The older woman lifted the corner of her almost-always-present apron and dabbed at her eyes. "Oh, pshaw, Cookie. *You* were the joy. You, and the hundreds and hundreds of pupils who brought sunshine into our lives." She let the apron drop and turned to face her niece. "And now that all that mushy stuff is out of the way, what do you think of my Jake?"

Susannah set the swing in motion again as she laid her head against the pillow, deliberately avoiding her aunt's too-observant eyes. "I think that *your* Jake is a very nice, very intelligent, very long-suffering man who found himself stuck in the middle of a problem and who is now trying his best to get out of it without causing too much trouble. I also think, Aunt Bitzy, that he's going to cut down Emily. Maybe not tomorrow, or even next week. But Emily's coming down. Count on it."

She sat forward and took hold of Aunt Bitzy's small hands. "Do you know that he's a lawyer? He could slap you with an injunction, or whatever, any time he feels like it."

Aunt Bitzy tugged her hands free, then used one of them to pat at her slightly sagging gray bun. "Of course I know that, Cookie. He told me all about his work one day when he visited me as I was tree-sitting Emily. But he isn't *that* sort of lawyer. He represents actors and actresses and those rich people who pay to have shows put on Broadway. The *theater*, Cookie. Comedy, tragedy, high drama, beautiful music. The lights, the stars, the glamour! It's all rather romantic, actually."

"Uh-huh," Susannah murmured, realizing that this was going to be even more difficult than she had imagined. "And the *man*, Aunt Bitzy? What do you know about the man?"

The older woman lowered her voice to a conspiratorial whisper. "I think there's some mystery there, Cookie. Perhaps even tragedy. You sense it, too, don't you? The handsome widower and his young son, fleeing the big city for life in the suburbs. Rather like that movie. What was it called? Oh, yes. *Sleepless in Seattle*. Only poor, handsome, romantic Jake is suffering his insomnia in Allentown. We really have to help him, Cookie. I sensed it almost at once. Really."

Susannah took a deep breath, wishing she didn't have to say what she knew must be said. Aunt Bitzy was as transparent as her sparkling-clean window-panes.

She might be out to save Emily, but she wasn't above—or beneath—a smidgen of matchmaking while she went about her crusade. A nice, *romantic* man. And, she suspected, an adorable young son. A six-bedroom house being built directly behind Aunt Bitzy's, where the romantic hero, the adorable boy, and the beloved niece—and a few babies thrown in over the years—could live happily ever after.

Well, it wasn't going to work. Not in this lifetime! And Aunt Bitzy had to know that, straight from the get-go. Susannah had a nice, quiet, well-ordered life in Manhattan. All right, so maybe it was boring once in a while, but it was safe, secure.

She didn't need to get mixed up with a man like Jake Longstreet, whose life had been front-page news for so long. Even now, with the scandal years behind him, he lived a public life. That was his job. That was his choice. But it wasn't the sort of life she, Susannah Yardley, would ever choose.

"Aunt Bitzy, I didn't remember all of it at first—I didn't remember the worst parts until we were half-way through dessert, as a matter of fact—but Jake was really making headlines for a while a few years ago. He was married to Jennifer Merchant—the Broadway star, and a real piece of work—and their custody battle for Alex during their divorce action was pretty hot. I mean, there was all sorts of dirty laundry being hung out in the tabloids. Then Jennifer died in a private plane crash in Aspen or someplace, and Jake just kind of disappeared from the society gossip columns, almost as if he'd dropped off the face of the earth."

"Oh, dear me. How sad!"

"Yes, Aunt Bitzy, it was. The only reason I remembered Jake's name was that I was surprised to read about some pretty public legal maneuvering he performed last year. After that, his name started popping up in the society columns again, and the old stories came out for another airing. Aunt Bitzy, I think Jake came to Allentown to keep Alex away from the gossip about his mother. Jake said he's nine now. Just the right age to start hearing things he shouldn't have to hear."

The ensuing silence was broken only by the soft chirping of crickets and the rhythmic squeak of the old metal swing as it glided back and forth on its equally ancient rollers. Susannah's aunt had her thinking cap on again, and her niece wasn't sure she wanted to hear what the woman might say next.

"Poor Jake," Aunt Bitzy said sadly, shaking her head. "Poor Alex. So all alone, two against the world. They're both very much in need of a happy ending, aren't they?"

Susannah covered her nervous laugh with a cough. Oh, yeah. Her aunt was up to something, all right, and it didn't take three guesses to figure it out. Her plan might have to take a left turn now that she had more information, but Susannah had no doubt the darling old conniver would soon figure out a way to keep to the main objective. Unless she, Susannah, applied the brakes—now.

"Yes, Aunt Bitzy, I imagine they are. But I don't have a leading part in this romance novel you're concocting in that lovely, sweet brain of yours. And, if you'll let me rather bluntly get to the point of this conversation, Jake has a snowball's chance in hell of giving Alex a quiet life here if you keep up with this business of tree-house-sitting. Every day another story appears in the local papers, the greater the risk that the national news may pick up on it. And you know what that means, don't you? It means that Jake will have moved Alex to Allentown and still not escaped the old gossip."

Aunt Bitzy stopped the swing with her foot, then stood, looking down at Susannah. "And you think it would be my fault? Well, how was I supposed to know all that, Cookie?" she demanded, hands on hips.

"I'm sorry for it, truly I am, but I had to do something to save Emily. I *promised* her. I even promised your uncle Frank when I went to the cemetery to discuss the problem with him. You wouldn't want me to go back on my word to your uncle, would you?"

"Aunt Bitzy," Susannah said as calmly and as evenly as she could, "Emily is a tree. Uncle Frank is in heaven, where all is forgiven, right? However, Jake and his son are real, living, breathing, vulnerable people. There's no comparison. Knowing what we know now, we can't allow this to continue. We can't let the national news find out about it. The television tabloid shows. You understand that, don't you? Aunt Bitzy? You're not listening to me. You're *tapping*. Oh, please, Aunt Bitzy. Don't *tap*. Dad always says that your tapping is like a storm warning, and we'd all better head for the basement before the tornado strikes."

Aunt Bitzy continued tapping her index finger against the side of her nose in the measured rhythm of a beating metronome, something she did when she was concentrating especially hard. "No, Cookie. Emily must remain standing. My mind is quite made up on that. But I do see your point about the reporters. Nasty people, by and large, although David, Stephen, and even Edward have been nothing but kind. They like to write happy stories too, you know, Cookie. Ones with lovely, happy endings. Wouldn't it be nice for everyone to open their newspaper one fine morning and discover a *happy* story? Now excuse me, for it's getting late, and I have to be up and back in Emily early tomorrow. Sleep on it, Cookie.''

Susannah was thoroughly confused now. "Sleep on what, Aunt Bitzy? I'm afraid you've lost me.''

The older woman sighed, then replied in her best patient-schoolteacher tones: "On how we're going to make this into a nice, lovely, *happy* story, of course. All good stories need conflict, Cookie—I read that somewhere when I was thinking of writing my own romance novel some years ago, shortly after your uncle Frank died and I was looking for a way to ease my grief. If there is no conflict, you see, no scandal, there is no story for any of those horrible tabloid shows and the like. So ours has to be a happy story, a boring, happy story, and then they'll all just go away, leaving Jake so happy himself that he'll forget all about doing away with poor Emily. Even David, Stephen and Edward will be happy, for they are good men, and seem truly interested in Emily.''

"Oh, yeah, Aunt Bitzy, I see your point," Susannah quipped, not seeing it at all. "Happy, happy. Everybody's happy. Oh, brother,'' she ended under her breath. What was that line from *Man of La Mancha*, one of her favorite musicals? Oh, yes. "I can hear the cuckoo singing in the cuckooberry tree.'' Only this tree was named Emily, and the cuckoo was her sweet, adorable, well-intentioned aunt.

Aunt Bitzy figuratively pinned the sadly smiling Susannah to the back of the swing, and back to attention, with her sudden, steely stare. "This alters my plans considerably, you know. And I had so wanted to be subtle. But do you think you could manage to have Jake fall in love with you within a week, Cookie—ten days at the most? Before these television tabloid people you spoke about can get wind of the story? Get wind of—that's a term used in Westerns, I believe. Or is that crime stories? Anyway, I had hoped we'd be halfway there by now—you and Jake in love, that is—but you certainly took your time in showing up, until I nearly sent you another letter. But I have every faith in you, Cookie.''

''Have him—have Jake fall in *love* with me? Well, color me surprised. You're wrong, Aunt Bitzy, you couldn't be subtle if you *tried*. I already figured out that you were planning on a little matchmaking. I just didn't take it seriously. But I sure don't understand what you're getting at now, with this business about heading the tabloids off at the pass. What possible good would it do to have Jake fall in— Lord! I can't even say the words again! Aunt Bitzy, I understand what you're trying to do for Emily, and I love you dearly—honestly, I do—but I think you've lost it this time. Really lost it!''

''No, I haven't,'' Aunt Bitzy said in the same rational tone she used to explain her reasons for naming her collection of African violets after the dwarfs in *Snow White*.

''If we can't keep the gossipmongers at bay,'' she continued, ''at least we can eliminate the measure of conflict and give them a happy ending. All is forgotten, all is forgiven, if we have that. A happy ending. And what better happy ending than two people finding true love? And, of course, Emily will be saved in the process, for I know you wouldn't let Jake have her cut down. Why, you could even recite your vows in the tree house. Isn't it wonderful how it is all working out?''

"Recite our vows in the tree— Wait a minute! Wait just one gosh-darned minute!'' Susannah called after her aunt as the woman scooted away, heading for the door to the kitchen as if she was the fairy godmother in *Cinderella* and was off to turn a lowly pumpkin into a glittering coach. "You can't drop a bomb like that and then just leave me here. Where do you think you're going now?''

Aunt Bitzy turned back for a moment, her smile beatific, if slightly spacey. "Why, I'm going to go write the vows, of course. I tell you, Cookie, this is the most romantic thing to happen to me in years. And all because of your uncle Frank's tree house. Do you think it's part of God's grand design?''

"God's design? How? In what way?'' Susannah asked, feeling the beginnings of a headache behind her eyes.

"God's design, Cookie. A message from your uncle Frank, guiding me toward a happy, fulfilling future with my beloved Cookie close by and another young life to cheer mine? I thought so, the first moment I saw Jake and Alex looking at their new house. I thought—what a wonderful idea for a romance novel! And with my own dear Cookie as the heroine. And then, when Jake announced he would cut Emily down— Well, never mind. I'm off!''

''There is that possibility, Aunt Bitzy,'' Susannah ruefully uttered under her breath, giving the old swing another push with her big toe as she wondered if it was too late to send out an SOS to her father in Florida.

4

Jake attempted to hit himself on the back as he coughed, having choked on his orange juice. "Wh-what did you say?" he managed at last, using his napkin to wipe at his slightly tearing eyes.

He had been about to enjoy a solitary breakfast on the patio when Susannah Yardley had appeared through the trees, brightening an already sunny morning, a picture of youth and beauty in her one-piece yellow romper that left an admirable amount of her equally admirable legs bare.

Even her blond hair, pulled back in a ponytail at her nape, seemed innocently sexy.

She was, in short, a sight to make his tired eyes—eyes that had spent more than half the night working on a complex legal brief—come alive again. But when she had opened that lovely mouth, and said what he felt pretty sure he had heard correctly, Jake had unexpectedly discovered a figurative fish bone in his orange juice.

"I *said,* Aunt Bitzy wants me to make you fall in love with me within a week—ten days at the outside,"

Susannah repeated from her chair on the other side of the round metal table that rested on the brick patio of Jake's rented house.

"Okay." Jake took another sip of juice. "That's what I thought you said. Now, if I could only figure out *why* you said it, I might yet die a happy man."

"I wouldn't bet on it," Susannah said, looking out over the lawn, toward the nearly completed house several hundred yards away. "As a matter of fact, I'd be willing to give you odds that *happy* is the last word you'll use to describe how you feel about Aunt Bitzy's plans. Tell me, do you always have your breakfast served to you on a silver platter?"

Jake lifted the silver dome and ladled another scoop of scrambled eggs onto his plate, then transferred two slices of bacon to the plate in front of him. "Only on alternate Saturdays. The rest of the time I prefer gold plate. Want some? Maria—that's my housekeeper—always makes enough to feed an army."

Susannah shook her head. "No, thanks. Aunt Bitzy must also have gotten her culinary training by cooking for the troops. I had to force down that last blueberry pancake before she took off for the treetops, carrying a basket of goodies with her. I understand she and your son are planning some sort of picnic for this afternoon."

Jake raised his eyebrows as he grimaced. "This is their third weekend together," he said, his appetite suddenly gone. "I go in to Manhattan two days a week until about ten o'clock, Alex has day camp every weekday, and now he spends his weekends with good old Aunt Bitzy. I hardly see the kid anymore, and when I do he's too busy chewing me out for trying to cut Emily down to really talk to me.''

Susannah was fiddling with the cutlery again, Jake noticed, happy to see that she wasn't quite as cool and composed as she would like him to believe—as her sleek, blond exterior would certainly lead him to believe.

And why should she be, after what she had told him? He'd allowed her to change the subject for a moment, but it was time he pushed her for an explanation. ''About this falling-in-love business, *Cookie*—''

''I'm sorry if Alex has gone over to the enemy, Jake,'' she said quietly, her eyes lowered so that her lashes cast intriguing shadows against her smooth, lightly tanned cheeks. ''I'm sure his defection is only temporary.''

He shrugged, then went after her again, in his best lawyer fashion. ''Yeah, well, that's life, and Alex is a sensible kid. We'll be all right. But to get back to this business of you making me fall in love with you. How do you plan to go about this assignment? Seduction seems a viable option, and one I'm open to, I suppose, if you don't mind me leading the witness a little,'' he ended, smiling as he watched her cheeks turn a becoming pink.

He allowed his smile to fade as Susannah quickly explained the reasoning behind Belinda Yardley's bizarre suggestion. She ended by saying, "I suspected from the beginning that she was up to some sort of matchmaking, but now she's acting as if she's on some sort of heavenly mission."

"I see," Jake said at last, pushing his plate away as he stood, jamming his clenched fists deep into the pockets of his tan slacks. "I thought you'd finally recall where you had heard my name—and not just because of *Remembering Mavis*. So you told your aunt all about Jennifer, about Alex's mother? Do you really think that was necessary?"

"Yes, yes, I do— I mean, I *did*," Susannah answered, also rising, and falling into step with him as he long-leggedly cut across the yard, heading for his unfinished house. "And I still would, which you would as well, if you'd stop to think about it, if things had only worked out the way they should have."

Was the woman speaking English? "How so?" Jake kept walking, figuring that it was better than standing still and maybe throwing something.

Susannah had to nearly break into a run to keep up with him, so that her voice was rather breathless as she continued earnestly: "Once I remembered the business about your former wife and all of that, I knew immediately that Aunt Bitzy had to be told. I had to tell her, warn her, because heaven only knows what she might have said if some reporter told her and she then just blurted out the first thing that came into her mind. You heard what Aunt Bitzy said about that reporter—the one with the deviated septum? I couldn't let that happen. So, if only for that one reason, I'm happy I told her."

"All right. And you're *not* glad you told her because—?" Jake prompted her as she paused to catch her breath.

"Well, that's simple, isn't it, considering what I already told you? I thought, if I explained everything to Aunt Bitzy, explained it rationally, she'd let you cut down Emily now, today, and there wouldn't be a story anymore. But almost the moment I said it, I realized it was only wishful thinking. So that's why I thought I was doing the right thing—right up until the moment I did it, if you can understand that."

"Reporters. They're like bulldogs, Susannah," he told her as he took her arm, helping her over the uneven ground near the house. "They never let go. Oh, they might look away for a moment or two, but they're always there, their teeth poised over your leg, ready to bite into the bone. Jennifer's been dead for seven years—long enough for Alex to have forgotten he even had a mother, not that Jennifer was ever much of a mother to him, poor kid."

"I'm so sorry, Jake," Susannah said, adding, "and thank you for slowing down. I think I was beginning to hyperventilate."

He smiled down at her. "Sorry. But you were right to consider what the national gossips might do if they saw my name connected to a story about Emily. I've already thought about them. If I can't keep your aunt out of the local newspapers, and if you're right, and

Madonna took the week off, it's all going to be dredged up again sooner or later. Marilyn Monroe's been dead for over thirty years, and they're still doing stories on her. Those television tabloid shows recycle more garbage than ten trash-to-steam plants.''

"And all because of my nearly forgotten childhood tree house," Susannah said sadly. "Again, Jake, I'm so very sorry."

Jake was a big boy now. He had been for a lot of years, having entered a highly public, highly charged profession, and having had the last of his naiveté stripped away the day he'd realized his beautiful, vibrant wife had the morals of an alley cat. He had known the moment the first reporter showed up at the tree house that his past might eventually be discovered and then dragged out into the open for another airing.

He could have cut the tree down that same day, and would have, if it hadn't been for Alex. His son had fallen in love with Belinda Yardley the moment the two had met, the motherly woman just the sort Jake would have picked as Alex's grandmother if he could have had that option.

Cutting down Aunt Bitzy's tree before he could make Alex see reason would have crushed the boy, who had hated the idea of moving to Allentown in the first place. Now that he had found a friend in his new "Aunt Bitzy," Alex had begun to unbend a little, had even agreed to the day camp.

No, Jake knew he had no choice in the matter. He had to allow Aunt Bitzy her crusade to save the tree house, even if it meant the possibility of a little bad publicity for himself.

He led Susannah across the large brick patio and opened one of the pair of French doors, motioning for her to precede him into the large family room. "Now, let's see if I have this right. Mrs. Yardley—dear old Aunt Bitzy—thinks that if the worst should happen, and one of those TV tabloid shows comes here, only to find that you and I are in love, then—" He stopped, confused.

"Then the story will have no *conflict,* but only a very boring happy ending, and the sleazy reporters will simply fold up their cameras and slink away, leaving me—your dearest beloved—to convince you that Fred is a jerk and the tree house would be a great place for a private wedding ceremony."

"Interesting concept," Jake said, smiling.

"And she only thought it up on the spur of the moment," Susannah told him. "Although she had already planned on my femme fatale talents making mincemeat of your heart, which is why she sent me a letter telling me about Emily in the first place. She didn't want moral support. She wanted me to come racing to Allentown and have you fall in love with me. The last bit, about heading off the gossip reporters at the pass with a happy story, was only thrown in last night. Quite an imagination for an old elementary-school teacher, don't you think? Did I tell you Aunt Bitzy loves romance novels?''

She hesitated, her expression earnest as she placed a hand on his forearm. ''Look—you get the ax, and I'll meet you under the tree house at midnight. It's the only way.''

''Oh, I don't know,'' Jake said, grinning at Susannah's obvious discomfort. ''I kind of like the idea, personally. Your aunt is right, there's nothing like a boring, happily-ever-after story to turn off the tabloid sharks' midfeeding frenzy. We could meet them together—in front of the tree house, of course—and serve them homemade brownies and glasses of milk. You could be wearing a dress you'd sewn yourself, and I could offer a homeowner's advice on getting rid of unsightly crabgrass. The reporters would all be out of here like a shot.''

''Very *unfunny*, Jake,'' Susannah replied with a snap, then brushed past him to enter the house. ''Oh! This is lovely! That ceiling must be nearly three stories high. And even a loft! I didn't realize. I can't see that wall of windows from my bedroom, you understand. And would you look at that *fireplace!* It's perfect!''

She turned to him, her green eyes fairly dancing. ''Don't curtain those windows, Jake. There's nothing beyond them except that fabulous view of the trees, and it would be criminal to cover that classic oriel design. Do you have a grand piano? A piano would be great in here.''

Remembering that Susannah was an interior decorator, Jake just nodded, enjoying the undiluted pleasure in her face. "A Steinway, that belonged to my maternal grandmother. I have it in storage right now. Anything else?"

She looked around the large room, speaking, it appeared to Jake, just as the words occurred to her. "The exterior design is classic Georgian for the most part, all weathered brick and, I suppose, white trim, once it's finished. Six bedrooms, you said. Oh, but this is the focal point, the real heart of the house. I'd paint this room cream—a thick, rich cream," she declared, seeming to look through him as she spoke.

"And since it will be a bright room even though it never gets direct sunlight, I'd go for greens, and blues, with dashes of cream and— No! You're not the cool blues-and-greens sort, are you, Jake? A good Oriental carpet—several of them, scattered around. Pick up the color scheme from the carpets. Dark, rich colors—and then the creams. The furniture? Eclectic. Antiques mixed with brasses and glass. And lots of plants."

As she spoke she turned this way and that, using her expressive hands to point out where the furniture would be, where she would place the plants. Jake could already see the room coming together in her mind, and in his.

"You're hired," he said flatly, taking her arm and leading her toward the archway that led to the remainder of the first floor.

* * *

"Oh, that was fun," Susannah said as they left the house the way they had entered, and she fairly skipped across the brick patio, knowing she should check on her aunt.

She stopped just at the edge of the bricks and turned to look at Jake. "And even though I know you were kidding about hiring me, I enjoyed every minute of it. Sort of a busman's holiday, I guess you'd say. The kitchen is going to be marvelous. The dark green marble for the countertops is just right. Perfect!"

Jake slipped his hands into the pockets of his slacks, a habit of his that she already recognized and found oddly endearing. And he had been so nice to her during their tour of the house; nice enough that she had forgotten all of Aunt Bitzy's silliness, even forgotten to feel embarrassed around him, threatened by him.

But now that her "cook's tour" was over, and he was standing in front of her, his nonthreatening pose so threatening to her sanity, she was beginning to feel decidedly uncomfortable.

"I wasn't kidding earlier, Susannah," he said, making her wish he didn't look so damned handsome as he squinted in the sunlight, a lock of dark hair falling forward over his forehead. "I want to hire you to decorate the house. The builder promised me it will be ready for occupancy in less than a month—sooner now that you've chosen the colors for the paint and wallpaper."

"Oh, but I couldn't!" Susannah exclaimed, hating herself for having to say no. "I have commitments in New York. Mrs. Thorogood is sure to come back from the Hamptons as soon as this heat wave is over, and—"

"Cindy Thorogood?" Jake interrupted. "I'll phone her. She'll understand. Besides, waiting for that woman to make up her mind about anything takes a lot more than a month. Who else?"

Susannah lightly bit on the soft inside of her left cheek. "Dozens," she said flatly, lying through her teeth, for Mrs. Thorogood's Fifth Avenue condo was her only commission at the moment. "More than you can count."

Jake's smile was so knowing, so confident, she wanted to slug him. "And would all these people be offering you the commission to do an entire house? Any way you wanted to do it? And with a fairly unlimited budget?"

"No," Susannah answered sarcastically, "they wouldn't be offering all that. But artistic freedom isn't everything."

"But it's pretty good to go on with, I'd say," Jake answered. "Remember, I work with some of the most creative people in the world. There are damn few of them who'd turn down the chance to call their own shots on a creative project."

"I knew I never liked lawyers," Susannah grumbled, looking up at the impressive wall of windows that had first caught her interest. "They're all such know-it-alls, and they have ways of saying things that make you afraid to lie to them." She redirected her gaze at Jake and smiled. "I guess I can't take the Fifth on this one, can I?"

"The truth, the whole truth, and nothing but the truth, Miss Yardley," he responded, his blue eyes twinkling. "Would you like to undertake a project where you have full freedom, a deep budget, and the chance to visit with your aunt for at least a month? Yes or no, Miss Yardley?"

Susannah could feel her palms itching at the thought of creating an entire house from the walls out, whole rooms built around themes that had been growing inside her head ever since design school.

All those fascinating rooms she could already see in her head! A media room. Two staircases, a graceful, curving one in the foyer and another leading up from the kitchen. A three-room office wing above the large garage. A sprawling master suite larger than her entire apartment. And Jake—working with him, consulting with him, seeing him day in, day out, for an entire month.

Oh, Lord, how she ached to say yes!

"What—what about Aunt Bitzy?" she asked quietly, avoiding Jake's eyes. If she was going to think rationally, she couldn't look into those hypnotic blue eyes. "If I say yes to this, she'll be picking out china patterns for us faster than you can say, 'Off with Emily's head.'"

"Very funny, Susannah." Jake smiled. "I think I can resist the temptation to succumb to your charms—if you can resist mine?"

Susannah pulled a face. "It'll be tough, all right," she said flatly, "but I think I'll be able to manage it, seeing as how I've never had any great fondness for arrogant, autocratic—"

"Then you'll take the job?" Jake interrupted, motioning for her to begin walking across the work site and toward the tree house. "I'll provide you with a list of the furniture that I've put into storage locally—as I've already sold my apartment in Manhattan. You'll be able to examine the furniture on Monday or Tuesday, once I call the storage office and set it up. Is that all right with you?"

It was. And he knew it, damn him. "I work on commission, Mr. Longstreet. Fifteen percent of the cost of the project. With a small retainer up front, to cover my expenses," she added, remembering that the rent on her apartment was due in two weeks.

"Will five thousand cover it, Miss Yardley? Separate from your fee, of course."

She nearly tripped over a small rock, so that he took her hand as they walked the rest of the way over the rough dirt that had yet to be prepared for landscaping. "Um—yes. Yes, of course. That should be sufficient." Visions of paying off all her credit cards began dancing in her head.

"Good. But only if we can be friends," he said, waving to the two occupants of the tree house.

"But if we're to have a professional relationship," Susannah protested, "I think it best to—"

"Friends, Susannah—or no deal. Now smile pretty, Cupid's watching. We wouldn't want her to think we're having our first lovers' quarrel."

"Lovers' quarrel?" Susannah couldn't have smiled if she'd just won the lottery. "You can't be serious! I won't pretend a romance to save your hide, for one thing—even if every tabloid television show in America sent crews here to dig up dirt on your past. And for the second thing—I wouldn't want to give Aunt Bitzy the impression that her silly romantic notions have any chance of success. Why, it would break her heart if—"

"All right, all right, I get the point," Jake interrupted. He interrupted her a lot, and she didn't think she liked it, even when he was saving her from her own big mouth.

He took hold of her arms, turning her to face him. "Look, I was only joking, and I admit the joke fell flat. The last thing I need, now or ever, is any sort of romantic attachment, even if I want to kiss you so much right now that I ache with the wanting. I tried romance and all that goes with it once and it didn't pan out, remember? Just work for me, Cookie. Get my new house ready for Alex and me, and help me get your wonderful, pain-in-the-neck aunt the hell out of that tree house before the whole world descends on my neck, okay?"

Cookie? He had called her Cookie. And she had liked it. Almost as much as she had liked hearing that he wanted to kiss her.

Susannah nodded, not trusting her voice, then headed for the tree house, wondering if her Aunt Bitzy had any idea of how very, very romantic her dark, mysterious, autocratic, arrogant latest hero, Jake Longstreet, really was.

5

Susannah was still in a rather disconcerting daze of mingled delight and apprehension as she approached the tree house, only to be shocked as she looked up to see her aunt sitting on the tree-house porch, an angel beside her.

It wasn't an angel, of course, which her second look confirmed, but the child came darn close. A thick shock of hair more white than gold. A high natural color in his boyish cheeks. Eyes so big and blue she could fall into them and never wish to be rescued. A beatific smile that could melt the hardest, most determined heart.

And a leather thong tied around his forehead, a huge feather sticking up from the back of his cherubic head.

"Hi, Dad!" the angel called out—Alex Longstreet called out—waving a hand that held an evil-looking rubber ax. "Look what Aunt Bitzy gave me. I'm an Indian. A *real* Indian! I'm learning all about the Lenni-Lenape, the Indians who lived right here hundreds of years ago. This isn't your tree, Dad. It belongs to the Indians, the Native Americans. And they were great. Noble and honest and heroic, Aunt Bitzy says. The Native Americans didn't believe in anybody owning anything, or fencing in land or anything, so Emily really belongs to nobody, and nobody can cut her down. Isn't that right, Aunt Bitzy?''

Susannah turned to Jake, who was running a hand through his hair. "I think you'd better pull out all your law books on this one, Counselor," she suggested, grinning. She might not want to become involved with Jake Longstreet, but she was already more than willing to fall in love with his son.

"Nice try, champ," Jake responded, "but it won't work. You do look great, though, doesn't he, Susannah?''

"He looks wonderful," Susannah said softly, realizing that, although Alex had his father's eyes, his coloring was all his mother's—the beautiful peaches-and-cream complexion, the white-blond hair. Looking at him, Jake must ache with both love and regret. Lord knew, it would take a harder heart than hers to ever wish to see those huge blue eyes cloud with unhappiness.

She took two steps toward the tree house, saying, "I'm Susannah Yardley, Alex, Aunt Bitzy's niece. It's nice to meet you."

Alex's smile broadened, showing white even teeth that looked just a little too large for his mouth, although she was convinced he'd "grow" into them, for he had long legs and showed every sign of someday being as tall as his father.

"I know," he told her. "And Emily is your tree house. Is it true that you and Uncle Frank sometimes slept out here? Aunt Bitzy says you did, with you and your friends up here and Uncle Frank sleeping on the ground, guarding you. I'll bet it's neat up here at night, with all the stars and stuff."

"And all the mosquitoes," Jake reminded, nudging Susannah lightly in the ribs, wordlessly telling her to downplay the thrill of tree-house sleeping.

She decided to help him out. "It was okay, I guess, Alex," she said, looking sternly at her aunt, who really was incorrigible, to be encouraging the child to such risky adventuring. "But your dad's right. Boy, do those bugs, and spiders, and weird things ever come out at night! Why do you think Aunt Bitzy doesn't sleep in Emily?"

The cherubic face turned mulish, a full bottom lip pushing forward in a pout. "Because Dad made a deal with her, that's why. He thinks if he pretends to be nice, that Aunt Bitzy will get tired of staying up here and let him cut Emily down. But she won't, and I won't, either. I love Emily!"

"Excuse me while I go get my black hat," Jake whispered out of the corner of his mouth. "That is what the villain wears in old politically incorrect cowboy-and-Indian movies, isn't it?"

"Not exactly number one on Alex's hit parade, are you, Jake?" Susannah commented quietly, her sympathies more with the father than the son. "I can see now why you haven't just gone ahead and cut Emily down. It could scar your relationship with Alex for life."

"That's what it says in all the parenting books, I suppose," Jake answered, jamming his hands in his slacks pockets yet again, probably to hide the fact that he had drawn them up into tight fists. Really, the man could use some relaxation, some peace and relative quiet. Building a house, uprooting himself from Manhattan, trying to settle into a new way of working, and commuting—all while striving to communicate with a motherless child. It was a lot to deal with, and she didn't envy him.

"Cookie, are you coming up to visit?" Aunt Bitzy, who had been busy watching the interchange between father and son, her brow furrowed, said at last. "We're going to weave mats out of some rattan I found in the attic yesterday, then start on *Huckleberry Finn.* It should be great fun."

"Um, no, thank you, Aunt Bitzy," Susannah replied hesitantly, eyeing the thick wooden "porch" critically, only to see several of the "frost cracks" Jake had mentioned etched on the trunk just below the flooring. "I think two for the tree house is enough. But I am going to keep myself busy. You see, Jake just hired me to decorate his new house."

Aunt Bitzy's smile on hearing this piece of news was so warm and fuzzy, so infused with happiness and hope, that Susannah had to look away.

Jake must have seen that smile, too, and interpreted it correctly. Leaning closer to Susannah's ear, he whispered, "Again, I'd say seduction is your best shot. After all, you wouldn't want to disappoint Aunt Bitzy."

"Oh, shut up!" Susannah exclaimed, not caring who heard her, and turned on her heel, heading for the back porch of Aunt Bitzy's house.

"She's a good girl, Jake, but she can be volatile. She takes that from her mother's side of the family, you understand," Susannah heard her aunt apologize behind her departing back, which only served to hasten her steps toward the house.

And she nearly made it, too, only to have Jake slip into the kitchen behind her before the old wooden screen door banged shut.

"Go away," Susannah ordered, pulling open the refrigerator door and sticking her head inside, knowing she'd find a pitcher of iced tea—which she would gladly dump over Jake Longstreet's head if he didn't do as she had ordered.

"Furthermore," she continued hotly, slamming the refrigerator door shut on the container of iced tea—and temptation—as she wheeled about sharply to face him, "you can take your cushy, creative-freedom decorating job and—"

She never had the chance to complete the sentence her aunt Bitzy would have had her writing an essay about if that woman had chanced to hear her dear niece utter it.

Susannah didn't have a chance to do much of anything, as a matter of fact, for the next thing she knew, Jake was holding her, kissing her, and the only coherent thought to form in her head as she slipped her arms around his narrow waist was that it certainly had taken the confounded man long enough to get to the point!

He tasted of freshly squeezed orange juice and smelled of cool, fragrant summer mornings. His lean body was hard beneath his shirt, his lips were soft against her own.

Susannah gave herself up to the rapidly deepening kiss, to the sweet sensations racing through her, to the straight-out-of-one-of-her-aunt's-beloved-books *romance* of the thing.

And then, just as she wondered what would happen next, Jake broke the kiss, smiling down at her as he cradled her within the circle of his arms. "Like I said, Susannah," he whispered, his voice an amused growl, "I've been wanting to do this for a while. Not bad. Not bad at all."

Susannah pushed herself out of his arms. "Yeah, I'll bet," she said, avoiding his eyes as she hugged herself, trying to pull herself back together after having felt as if she had been shattered into a million small, painful pieces. "I'd give it an eighty-five myself. Long on expertise, but a little short on commitment."

His deep-throated chuckle only added fuel to the fire of her rapidly growing anger. "Commitment? I thought I was kissing the niece, not the aunt. Or are you both incurable romantics?''

Eyes narrowed, Susannah glared at him. "Don't try so hard, Jake. I can dislike you without much effort at all. The last thing you have to worry about with me is any sort of commitment. It's simply that I don't enjoy being used any more than you do. My aunt is at least well-intentioned, if misdirected. So no more kisses, all right? Aunt Bitzy wouldn't approve, as she is, as you say, a romantic. She doesn't understand male lust.''

He pushed a hand through his hair, holding it away from his forehead as he glared at her. "Oh, good. Good," he said, shaking his head. "Now I'm lusting after you? You got all that from one small kiss? You know what, Susannah? You and you aunt are *both* nuts. Certifiable!''

Susannah stamped her foot, immediately hating herself for the action, which even the most melodramatic romantic heroines shunned. "How dare you insult my aunt!" she exclaimed, knowing she had just talked herself out of a valuable commission, a lovely monthlong visit in Allentown with her aunt, and the chance to get to know this intriguing man and his adorable son better.

"Look, Cookie—"

"And *don't* call me Cookie!" Susannah interrupted, wishing she had grabbed that container of iced tea when the grabbing was good.

"All right—Susannah." Jake backed up two paces, his hands outstretched in front of him as if to prove to her that he was harmless. "Let's take this from the top, shall we?"

She rolled her eyes. "Do we have to? Oh, all right, Counselor. Fire away."

"Point in evidence—you came to me this morning and informed me that your aunt had asked you to make me fall in love with you. Within the week, as I recall. Or, at the outside, within ten days. Am I correct so far?"

Susannah picked up a wooden spoon that had been lying on the countertop and began twirling it between her fingers. "So far," she said, looking up at him from beneath her lashes. "Go on."

"Second point of evidence. I told you, very matter-of-factly, very honestly, that one, I wanted to kiss you, and, two, that I had no thought of ever again forming a romantic attachment with anyone."

"And then you hired me to decorate your house," Susannah interjected, thinking she should be saying something. Anything. Even if it wasn't entirely relevant. How did she become the defendant, when he was the one who had committed the "crime"?

"A commission which you accepted," he reminded her, making it sound as if she had agreed to become his mistress or something.

"Your point?"

"I'm getting to it. We then went to the tree house, to see your aunt and my son. At which *point—*" he said the words as if he was about to announce that the butler did it "—you took one look at Alex and melted like vanilla ice cream in the sun. Do you know what that did to me?"

She shook her head, all thoughts of shouting "Sexual harassment!" fleeing her head. "No, Jake," she admitted honestly. "I have no idea what that did to you."

He raised a hand and rubbed at the back of his neck. "Neither do I," he said softly. "God, forgive me, Cookie. I can't explain it, either. I guess, just for the sake of argument, that for a moment—for enough moments for me to come in here after you and make a complete ass of myself—I bought into your aunt's little fantasy. We've been on our own for a lot of years, Alex and I. And now, in just a few short weeks, we've built a house, met Aunt Bitzy, and now you're here, and—"

If she had, as Jake had termed it, "melted" when she saw Alex, she knew herself to be a pure puddle of emotions now. "Oh, Jake, I'm so sorry!"

"Yeah," Jake said shortly, jamming his hands into his pockets. "So am I. And it won't happen again. I promise."

Then he smiled, and Susannah squeezed the handle of the wooden spoon with both hands, relaxing her grip only as she realized the wood might snap under the pressure. "All right, ladies and gentlemen of the jury. The verdict's in. Not guilty, by reason of temporary infatuation. Case dismissed."

He turned for the door. "See you later, Susannah."

"Whoa!" she called out, taking a single step to follow him. "Who's not guilty? You, or me? Because I did kiss you back, if you'll remember."

His smile was wicked, and terribly exciting. "Yes, you did, didn't you? A piece of evidence I've overlooked. I'll have to think about that one for a while, I suppose, then possibly appeal the verdicts. But, for the moment, I'd say neither of us is guilty. For the moment."

And then he was gone, the old wooden screen door slamming shut behind him, and Susannah leaned back against the countertop, letting out her breath in a relieved rush.

"Temporary infatuation," Jake had called the reason behind their kiss. It seemed a reasonable excuse, and blame for the "crime" could most certainly be laid firmly at the feet of her scheming, romantically-minded Aunt Bitzy.

They had been caught up in the fanciful, sweetly romantic aberration of her aunt's fertile mind, caught off guard by the pleasantness of the morning, and caught lacking in reason when it came to an explanation behind their sudden, unlooked-for attraction to each other.

However—and completely putting Aunt Bitzy's wishful thinking to one side—Susannah felt pretty sure that this silly little "romance" had at least a few more chapters to run before anyone could guess at the ending.

6

"Dad?"

Jake shook his head, trying to free himself of his thoughts, which had a lot to do with the way Susannah Yardley's long, slim body had felt when pressed closely against his, and precious little to do with the project at hand. "Yes, Alex?"

"I just asked you if I should press the Return key to post my message to this board," Alex told him patiently, sounding more like the parent than the child. "If my answer is the right one, I get three free hours of computer time next month. But I have to post the answer, and I don't know which key to press to enter it."

Jake leaned over his son's shoulder, reading the typed message that was Alex's answer to a complicated question about a shortcut to solving one of his on-line computer games. The on-line service was running a contest, and Alex was determined to win himself free time on the line. Not that Alex paid the monthly bill out of his allowance. It was just that Alex liked to win.

Takes it from his father's side of the family, Jake thought, remembering Belinda Yardley's explanation of Susannah's temper. "Yes, Alex," he said now. "Once you think you've got it, hit Return, and your answer is posted. And then, my boy, it is time for bed. *Past* time for bed. Okay?"

The small head nodded close beside Jake's cheek, the freshly washed white-blond hair tickling his skin. "I'm going now, Dad, 'cause I have to get up early tomorrow to tree-sit while Aunt Bitzy goes to church. You know, you could have given her Sundays off. But I guess, since we don't ever go to church except for Christmas and Easter and stuff, you didn't really think about it."

"I guess I didn't consider it, champ," Jake admitted, feeling as if he should be charged as an unfit parent. "Alex—would you like to go to church tomorrow morning?"

"With Aunt Bitzy?" the boy asked challengingly, sending Jake's spirits even lower. "What are you gonna do, Dad? Cut down Emily while we're gone?"

He rubbed at his son's head. "No. I'm going to take advantage of the fact that you're gone and see if I can clean up this room. Maria told me that, since I don't give her hazardous duty pay like she got when she was in the navy, she refuses to enter the area. Or maybe," he added, hoping he didn't sound desperate, "I could go to church with you?"

Alex turned off the computer and turned to look up at his father. "It's not some special religious holiday or anything tomorrow, is it?'' he asked, looking confused.

''Nope. I just think Aunt Bitzy's right. We should go to church every Sunday, not just on special days. So, what do you say?''

Alex assessed him through narrowed eyes. ''Will you want to sing?''

Alex sang beautifully, just like his famous mother. Jake, however, couldn't carry a three-note tune in a large bucket, and it was a family joke he and Alex shared. Hearing a reference to his failing now eased the tension between Jake's shoulder blades and he smiled, then blinked rapidly a few times, refusing to believe he had any problem other than a bout of allergies that was making his eyes water.

''Not a note, champ, I promise. I wouldn't want to get thrown out, now would I?''

Alex scrambled out of his chair and skipped across the room to launch himself into bed. ''Aunt Bitzy says she has to leave for church at nine-thirty. We can follow her and Miss Yardley, I suppose, if we meet them in front of their driveway. We could take them, except that dumb car only has room for the two of us. Not like Rachel. Rachel holds six people, you know. Even eight, if some of the people are little.''

''Everyone's a critic,'' Jake grumbled good-naturedly as he tucked in his son, remembering Susannah's comments about his low-slung sports car. ''I think I'm beginning to get a complex. My car doesn't even have a name.''

"Yes, it does, Dad," Alex told him, reaching up to kiss his father good-night. "Aunt Bitzy and I named it the other day. She said we should call it Raoul. That's French, I think she said."

"Raoul?" Jake covered his amusement with a slight cough. "Yeah, well, champ, I think we're going to have to call it something else soon, too. We're going to have to call it my commuter car. If we're here in Allentown for keeps, and I think we are, I'm going to have to start figuring out whether I want to pretend I'm a desert sheik or a spaceman."

"Huh?"

Jake walked to the doorway and put his hand on the light switch. "Well, if you're going to join a soccer team this fall, and I'm going to be driving you and your friends to games, I'll need a minivan. What kind do you want?"

Alex's smile was rather demonic for a cherub. "Ask Miss Yardley, Dad. Aunt Bitzy says she'll be driving me to practice. Just like all the other kids have their moms take them places."

Jake flipped off the light switch, sure he could still see in the darkened room. Eyes red with rage should be able to see in the dark, after all. "Aunt Bitzy told you that, champ?" he asked, trying to keep his voice low and controlled. "And when did she tell you that?"

"Well," Alex said slowly, seeming to sense that he had said something wrong, "she didn't actually *say* it, Dad. Aunt Bitzy was just making up a story one day while we were in the tree house. It was a neat story,

Dad, with the hero rescuing the beautiful woman from a tall, wooden tower and everyone living happily ever after in a great new house.''

"And from that you got that Miss Yardley will be taking you to soccer practice?''

"I guess you'd have to hear Aunt Bitzy tell the story, Dad,'' Alex said quietly, speaking through a yawn. "But I think I've got it right. Miss Yardley sure is pretty, isn't she? Her hair's a lot like mine, and she liked all the things I like now—chocolate-chip cookies, *Tom Sawyer*, Emily, Aunt Bitzy.''

"And now, I suppose, *Huckleberry Finn*,'' Jake murmured, almost to himself.

"Yeah. I'm doing all the things Miss Yardley used to do when she was little. I liked her picture when Aunt Bitzy showed it to me, and I like her even better now that she's come to save Emily. Do you like her, Dad, or are you mad at her for trying to save her tree house? I don't think you could be mad at her, or else you wouldn't have let her decorate our new house, which is just what Aunt Bitzy said you'd do.''

"Is that right?'' Jake grumbled, beginning to think Aunt Bitzy needed a fast lesson in reality—one he just might deliver in the form of Fred Gibbons and his chain saw.

"Uh-huh,'' Alex answered in all his childhood innocence. "You know something, Dad? I really hated it when you said we were moving here. But now—well, I think I really like it. I like it a whole lot. Thanks,

Dad. Don't forget to get me up early so we can go to church.''

"Church it is, champ," Jake agreed as affably as he could, then quit the room. They would all go marching merrily off to church in the morning. Alex. Aunt Bitzy. Susannah. And him. One big happy "family."

At which time I will most fervently pray for the strength to remember that Aunt Bitzy's fantasy has absolutely nothing to do with reality, he promised himself as he stared out the window, watching as a cool evening breeze gently rustled the topmost leaves of Emily the elm tree.

Susannah sat in the safe, cloaking darkness of the evening, slowly pushing the swing back and forth as she watched the parade of lights in the house across the way.

One by one the upstairs lights went out, with only the soft glow of what was probably a hall light still burning. One by one the lights on the ground floor came on, as Jake made his way downstairs.

Alex was in bed. His father was not.

What did he do all evening in his rented house, with his son asleep, and his housekeeper already in her room above the detached garages? Did he watch television? Did he work on legal papers or some such thing? Or did he sit, alone, and think?

Think about the past, and the life he had had, the life he had lost, the life he had left behind to move his child to the safety, the anonymity, of Allentown?

Jennifer Merchant had been so very beautiful. So lushly, curvingly petite; so blond, so vibrant, so *alive*.

Susannah had only been seventeen or so when Jennifer Merchant and Jake Longstreet had married. The Broadway star and the powerful lawyer. The queen of the musical stage and the scion of an old, monied Newport family, all now deceased. The angel and the devil's advocate, or so the tabloids had said.

For Susannah had been born and raised in Manhattan, born to parents who faithfully took her to every show on Broadway, from plays to musicals, to revivals of some of the perennial favorites that were recycled from time to time.

Susannah had loved the musicals best, and her scrapbook, containing more than a few pictures of Jennifer Merchant, was probably still packed up with the rest of her possessions that had moved to Florida with her parents.

It had been during Susannah's time in design school that the very public breakup of the fantasy marriage had come, and she could remember seeing pictures of Jennifer Merchant as she was being rushed into Lenox Hill Hospital after the first of several suicide attempts that had always seemed more staged than real.

But it was Jake's pursuit of total custody of their then infant son that had rocked all of the theater world, and most of the country as well, for Jennifer Merchant had just completed her first movie and was being touted as the next Marilyn Monroe. What was it Jake had said? Oh, yes. Something about Monroe having been dead for thirty years, which hadn't been long enough for all the stories to die.

But the stories about Jennifer Merchant and her penchant for other men's beds, other women's husbands, and risk-taking that had linked her for a time to both a major underworld gang boss and his alleged trafficking in drugs, had all ended with her death.

Ended, but not to be forgotten. Jake had done a good job of staying out of the limelight, keeping Jennifer Merchant's son out of the limelight, for more than half-a-dozen years, until his involvement in the flak over importing an English singer for a part in *Remembering Mavis*.

Not that any of the tabloids had mentioned Alex, thank goodness.

No, they had concentrated on publishing pictures of Jake and Jennifer together. Jennifer as seen in her starring roles on Broadway. Jennifer's private airplane smashed against a mountain face. Jake's dark presence at the side of the white, flower-bedecked casket the day of Jennifer's small, private funeral.

Susannah had never really paid much attention to the photographs of Jake Longstreet. How could she, when any photograph of Jennifer's gorgeous face seemed to put anyone else in the shade, leaving her alone in the sunlight of her startling beauty?

But Susannah had read about Jake Longstreet's return to Manhattan society's pages just this past winter; read about him, spared a moment to think about the old scandal, about the young child he was raising alone—and then forgotten it.

Until now. Jake Longstreet was real now, as was his son, Alex. They were real people, with real problems, and they had somehow become a part of her life: for the time it would take to solve the problem of Emily, for the month or more that it would take to decorate his house, for the years and years it would take her to forget his kiss.

Susannah sighed, amazed to find herself in the role of tragic heroine in Aunt Bitzy's romance, even as she told herself that she was nothing of the kind. It was a kiss. That's all. One kiss. It wasn't as if she hadn't been kissed before, because she had been. She had been made love to, by only one man; the wrong man, and that had been over for more than two years.

She wasn't some innocent virgin. She wasn't a heroine waiting to be rescued. And she certainly had nothing in common with any romantic young maiden in search of a happy ending.

She was a thoroughly modern woman. Independent. Emancipated. Liberated. Self-sufficient. Unencumbered . . . and liking it.

"And into it up to your eyebrows if you believe any of that garbage," she grumbled out loud, getting to her feet and walking away from the house, away from her thoughts, away from the memory of Jake's kiss. Away from Jake's admission that he, too, had been momentarily caught up in Aunt Bitzy's fantasy.

For more than an hour, as crickets chirped in the tall grass, as the lightning bugs blinked in the night, and as the lights in the house across the way slowly narrowed to the windows of one upstairs bedroom, Susannah sat on the small porch of the tree house, her knees drawn up against her chest, and wondered why, despite her precarious situation, the last thing she would ever consider would be to pack up her belongings and head back to Manhattan.

The very last thing she would ever consider...even though it was probably the wisest thing she could do.

7

Jake shepherded Alex ahead of him as the two Longstreet men followed Belinda and Susannah Yardley into the local pancake house, an after-church ritual Aunt Bitzy had graciously expanded to include her niece and new neighbors.

"Such a lovely sermon, wasn't it, Susannah?" Aunt Bitzy asked, eyeing Jake as she spoke. "I do so enjoy that theme. 'Love thy neighbor as thyself.' Alex, loosen your tie, dear, if you wish. Your behavior in church this morning was exemplary, and should be rewarded."

Alex looked quickly to his father for approval, then grinned and pulled off his clip-on tie, stuffing it in his pocket. "Good morning, Aunt Bitzy," a young waitress said as she approached them. "I see you have guests this morning. How lovely."

"Yes, Glynis, I'm very fortunate," Aunt Bitzy responded as she waved to a T-shirt-clad busboy who sported a half-shaved head and an earring. "Please tell Roger I don't approve, Glynis, dear," she added, still smiling at the young man. "I don't care if your baby brother is heading off to U.C.L.A. this fall—that earring has to go. His art is sufficient to make a statement, and he has no need of artifice!''

''Yes, Aunt Bitzy,'' Glynis replied, winking at Jake and Susannah as if to say they should understand that everyone enjoyed humoring the retired schoolteacher. ''I'll tell him. And I'll also tell him not to even think about getting another basket of your chocolate-chip cookies until his hair grows out. Now, what can I get you folks?''

They all placed their orders before Jake sat back, listening with only half an ear as Aunt Bitzy explained that Glynis and her brother Roger had both been her pupils, and that she considered her job unfinished until she saw all her students safely settled in the world.

A bit of a minor despot, Aunt Bitzy was, Jake decided ruefully, and quite determined in her fuzzy, doting ''good witch'' way. The woman was an irresistible mixture of love and concern and discipline, and it was no wonder that Alex had fallen under her spell.

It was obvious the woman genuinely wished the best for everyone, just as it was clear that she had no idea that she might be considered pushy when she involved herself in someone else's life.

But how could anyone be angry with her for long? She had a good, pure heart. Her motives were equally pure. And she certainly had done wonders for Alex in the three short weeks they had been in residence in Allentown.

However—and Jake knew it was a very large "however"—if he didn't soon apply the brakes to this lovely, velvet steamroller, he just might find himself in real trouble.

Looking toward Susannah, who was fiddling with the cutlery again, and listening to Aunt Bitzy chatter on about how marvelous it was that her beloved niece was "fitting so wonderfully well into the life here in Allentown," Jake decided that she must feel much the same as he did.

Aunt Bitzy was a doll, a real doll. She was also a master puppeteer, pulling the strings on those she wished to control and, for the most part, doing it very well.

But all the string pulling, and all the wishful thinking, weren't enough to make two people who barely knew each other instantly fall in love, marry, and secure Aunt Bitzy's romantic notions of "happily ever after."

Especially when neither of the parties involved particularly asked for any such happy ending.

All Susannah wanted was to visit with her aunt, fulfill her commission to decorate the new house, settle the business of Emily's fate, and get back to her career, and her life, in Manhattan.

All he, Jake, wanted to do was see his new house completed, spend more time with his son, and wave goodbye as Emily and the tree house were both carted off to the local dump.

That's all. No romance. No falling in love. No nothing. Period. Which, of course, certainly explained why he had kissed Susannah yesterday. Why he would like nothing better than to kiss her, hold her, again today. Oh, yeah. Sure, it did....

"Susannah, stop fiddling," Aunt Bitzy said quietly, and Jake looked into Susannah's eyes, then winked at her as she grimaced in much the same way Alex did when he was reprimanded.

Poor Susannah, Jake thought, unconsciously sitting up straighter before Aunt Bitzy could turn her critical eye on his relaxed posture.

As he readjusted his chair, he looked around the large restaurant only because it gave him something more natural to do than to continue wondering what Susannah would do if he moved his knee slightly to the left, so that it pressed lightly against hers.

And that's when he noticed it.

The stare.

The nudge.

The giggle.

He dropped his napkin onto the floor, then took the chance to take a quick look behind him as he picked it up.

More stares.

Another nudge.

Two giggles.

He knew all the signs because he'd seen them all before. Was that why Susannah was being so quiet? Had she noticed as well?

Now that he knew that their table had somehow become the center of attention, Jake could feel dozens of eyes figuratively staring a hole in his back. He could sense the keen interest, the titillated curiosity, the obvious enjoyment that swirled around him, all taken at his expense.

Damn it! What was the matter with people? Didn't anyone have any appreciation for someone else's privacy anymore?

Stupid question, Longstreet, he told himself as he watched Susannah bite her bottom lip, her cool, sea green eyes glittering with emotion as Aunt Bitzy and Alex, oblivious to what was going on all around them, talked about the chance of taking Rachel out for a drive later in the afternoon, perhaps even to Trexler Park to feed the ducks.

If Jake would be kind enough to allow her to fulfill her end of their arrangement by "visiting" Emily later in the day, Aunt Bitzy said, which he, of course, would. She didn't ask him—she told him. But very nicely.

"Susannah?" Jake asked quietly, leaning toward her as Aunt Bitzy informed Alex she was sure she had a good supply of day-old bread to feed the wild ducks. "Am I paranoid, or is everyone in this joint staring at us?"

"Unless there's a sword swallower or something performing behind us," she whispered back, "I'd say we're it. I feel like there's a spotlight over my head or something. I *hate* feeling conspicuous. What's going on?"

"I don't know," Jake answered honestly, "but I'm beginning to get a bad feeling about those reporters who were interviewing your aunt the day you got here. There is a Sunday paper in this town, you know. Sunday's always a good day for human-interest stories. Damn. I'm going to have to subscribe. All I get now is the *New York Times,* which clearly doesn't keep me as well-informed as I should be."

He watched as all the color left Susannah's cheeks, only to return in a hot, flattering blush. "The newspaper!" she whispered fiercely. "Of course! One of the reporters probably wrote about Aunt Bitzy's crusade to save the tree. Even worse, when Aunt Bitzy reads the story she'll be absolutely thrilled by all of it. And they're probably hating you because you want Emily cut down. Oh, Lord, why is there never a convenient hole to hide in when you want one?"

Jake could hardly believe it, but he felt a smile beginning to tug at the corners of his mouth. "Shall I give them all the infamous Longstreet legal-eagle stare? One of my more flamboyant clients once told me I could level the Empire State Building with a single glare."

"Not that I'm unimpressed, Mr. Kong—but, no, don't," Susannah responded, placing both hands in her lap as Glynis arrived with their orders. "Just eat fast and then let's get out of here. I want to get home to Aunt Bitzy's newspaper."

"We think as one, fair lady," Jake said, as a young wife sitting with her husband and two young children waved at him, then slipped her arms around her youngest child's shoulders and gave her a hug.

"Roger just showed me the front page of the local section, little guy," the waitress said as she slipped an oval plate bearing an enormous waffle decorated in a fresh-fruit and whipped-cream clown face in front of a bug-eyed Alex. "And you know what? I think you're a real sweetie. Here's hoping you get everything you want."

And then, as Jake looked on, also "bug-eyed," but not with awe at the waffle, Glynis gave Alex a kiss on the cheek. What was this—national hug-your-child day?

That's when Jake looked around the room once more and noticed that, although people had been staring—were still staring—not one of them was looking at him in the way people had when he and Jennifer were wrangling over custody of Alex.

These people didn't look nosy, or titillated by gossip.

They looked happy.

And genuinely interested; even pleased.

"Alex—" Jake began, hoping to learn something from his now whipped-cream-mustached child, just to have Aunt Bitzy cut him off.

"The breakfast table is no place for prolonged discussion, Jake," she instructed, looking at him levelly, warningly, so that he realized that, although Susannah had not seen the Sunday paper, Belinda Yardley obviously had.

"Now, as I was saying, Jake," she continued in her happy way, "Alex and I will take Rachel and go feed the ducks, while you and Susannah use your car to go back to the house to spend a leisurely hour or so reading the newspaper."

"Then you've already read—"

"I especially like the cartoons, don't you?" Aunt Bitzy interrupted as Susannah tried to question her. "Some of them have been around so long I feel like the characters are members of my family. If only that Cathy girl could learn to relax a little, I'm sure she could convince Irving to marry her. Her dog is cute enough, but once a spinster starts buying pets it's almost as if they've given up, don't you think? Susannah—you haven't adopted any cats or anything, have you?"

"No cats, Aunt Bitzy, although I was looking at a twelve-foot-long boa constrictor just last week," Susannah muttered from between clenched teeth, kicking Jake hard under the table when he forgot himself enough to laugh out loud.

When Alex pounced on the subject of pets, putting forth his well-known argument concerning the reasonableness of a nine-year-old boy being allowed his own cocker spaniel, the three adults allowed him to dominate the conversation until Glynis deposited the check on the table and they could, at last, escape the fishbowl that the dining room of the local pancake house had become.

"Go get him, honey," one blue-haired old lady whispered rather loudly as Susannah passed by her table on the way out of the restaurant, so that Jake found it difficult not to break the speed limit as he steered the sports car—Susannah sitting stiffly in the passenger seat—back to Aunt Bitzy's house.

Susannah was out of the car almost before it came to a full halt, her key already in her hand, her entire being centered on the mission of finding the local section of the Sunday newspaper and hiding in a locked bathroom until she could read every word of the story she was sure she would find.

The best-laid plans of mice and men never quite going as hoped, she could only watch in disgust as Jake bounded past her and opened the door she belatedly remembered her aunt saying hadn't been locked in thirty years.

Jake did stop long enough to usher her inside but, as she made a beeline for the kitchen table, he headed for the living room that was a pleasant clutter of overstuffed furniture and handmade lace doilies, exclaiming, "Aha!" just as she crossed the threshold into the kitchen.

"You found it?" she asked, sticking her head into the living room in time to see Jake collapsing onto the couch, a section of the newspaper clutched in both hands.

"You found it," she repeated a moment later as she sat down beside him and peeked at the front page only to see herself—mostly the *back* of herself as she climbed the steps toward the tree house—displayed in a large photograph above the fold.

The headline, she realized in mounting shame and anger, was no more flattering to her sense of herself as a mature woman of the modern world: Princess Climbs To Leafy Bower.

"What's *that* supposed to mean?" she asked angrily, poking a finger at the headline, then leaned even closer to read the caption beneath the photograph. "Susannah Yardley, a little boy's real-life fairy princess, defends her childhood tree house from certain destruction by Prince Charming."

She fell back against the pillows, dislodging one of Aunt Bitzy's doilies, which fell forward to cover her hair like a veil—or a crown?

"Damn that miserable, fibbing nail biter for snapping that picture," she groused after more than a full minute in which she could think of absolutely nothing to say. She looked at the page Jake was reading once more, then quickly closed her eyes yet again. "Damn him, damn the reporter, damn *all* reporters! How could they do this to me?"

"Welcome to the real world, Susannah," Jake said, laying the newspaper on his lap. "Reporters don't have to worry about who they hurt. They just report the facts—or their version of the facts. And, in this case, they seem to have had some help.''

She sat forward once more. ''What did Aunt Bitzy say to them? Surely she didn't fill them in on her whole scatterbrained idea about the two of us falling in love?''

''No,'' Jake answered, running a hand through his hair. ''At least not directly. *Alex* told them.''

''Alex?''

''You do remember the waitress, don't you? How she kissed that sweet, darling *big-mouthed* child of mine? How everyone was looking at us, and smiling like certifiable idiots, and hugging their own kids? God, Susannah, I'm surprised they didn't take up a collection for the ring.''

Jake neatly folded the newspaper, then threw it on the floor and got to his feet, walking over to the Priscilla-curtained front window and jamming his hands into his slacks pockets.

Much as she hated doing it, Susannah reached down and picked up the newspaper, avoiding looking at the sight of her bare legs and shorts-clad derriere as she began reading.

The first part of the story recounted Aunt Bitzy's crusade to save Emily and the tree house, but it was all glossed over very quickly before the reporter zoomed in on his interview with Alexander Longstreet, son of ''Emily's new owner.''

So much for worrying about some national wire service picking up on the fact that Jake Longstreet, lawyer, a man whose life was once fodder for the gossip mills, was up to his neck in trouble in Allentown, Pennsylvania. Why, Jake wasn't even named as being any more than Alex's father!

"'With the innocence of a child,'" she read aloud, "'Alexander Longstreet recounted to this reporter the history of Emily the tree house, and the fairy princess who lived there long ago. His Aunt Bitzy, as young Alex calls Belinda Yardley, beloved former elementary-school teacher of nearly three generations of Allentown residents, has told such wonderful stories of that long-ago "princess" that Alex began to believe that she would be the perfect person to bring a "happily-ever-after" into his life, and the life of his widowed father.'"

Susannah stopped reading and looked up at Jake in time to see a muscle begin to work in his jaw.

"'The beautiful princess and the sad prince,'" she continued, her heart pounding, "'the fairy godmother and the innocent child, and even the Disneylike tree with a personality and troubles of its own, have been thrown together in a fairy-tale story worthy of the movies. This reporter will continue to report the story until its conclusion, his fingers crossed that young Alex will be blessed with the thing he desires most—a happy ending.'"

Susannah laid the newspaper back on the floor and then slumped bonelessly against the couch cushions. "Oh, Lord," she said quietly, not knowing what else to say. "Oh, my good Lord."

"Your aunt wouldn't happen to have a birdcage we could line with that thing?" Jake asked, turning to face Susannah.

She shook her head, ruefully smiling in spite of herself. "What are you going to do now?"

"Excuse me?" he prompted, and she shivered slightly as he stared at her—probably using that Empire State Building-leveling stare he'd told her about. Heaven knew, she sure felt as if her legs had just been cut out from under her. "What am *I* going to do now? Isn't that, what are *we* going to do now?"

8

Susannah climbed to the porch of the tree house just as an orange-red sun dipped below the tallest of the oak trees in the backyard of Belinda Yardley's house, hoping to escape both her aunt's gentle smiles and the memory of Jake's angry glare as he had left her alone with the Sunday newspaper and slammed out the front door.

With her head bent so that she would not bump it on the doorway that had once seemed so tall—her portal into her childhood fantasies—she entered the tree house itself, smiling as she clicked on the battery-powered lamp and a thousand wonderful memories instantly assaulted her from every side.

The small, hand-hewn square table and lattice-back chairs still sat in the middle of the floor, settled against a braided oval rag rug Aunt Bitzy had fashioned from bits and pieces of cloth—all of which held more memories.

There was one six-inch-long section made out of the blue-and-white-striped dress Susannah had snagged on a fence nail when she was six.

The green-and-red plaid row of braiding had once been Uncle Frank's favorite flannel shirt, and the five-inch length of pink cotton had come from one of Aunt Bitzy's well-worn aprons.

All the once-adored pictures still hung from the walls, safe and secure inside frames her uncle had made in his workshop.

There was the coloring-book page she had colored—the one showing Snow White dancing in the forest, her cape held up by tiny bluebirds.

Another frame held a picture of Uncle Frank, his wrinkled, beloved face wreathed in a smile as he sipped pretend tea from a small white cup as he attended one of Susannah's tree house tea parties.

So many pictures. So much of her carefree, nearly idyllic youth, captured forever inside this one small space.

Her first attempt at needlepoint.

A crude drawing of Aunt Bitzy in the act of mixing up her chocolate-chip cookie batter—with the words "Aunt B. and Her Choclit Chits" scribbled across the bottom.

And there, on that shelf beneath one of the windows, stood the clay sculpture of Bo-Peep that Susannah had made at summer camp.

Susannah pressed a hand against her mouth as tears stung her eyes. Nothing had changed in all these years. Aunt Bitzy and Uncle Frank had kept it all here, kept it all safe. Her childhood. Wrapped up in Emily's loving arms and tucked into a time warp that kept Susannah forever that pigtailed blond ten-year-old, forever their special child.

But Susannah had come no more to the special enchanted childhood bower, leaving Emily and the tree house all alone, and waiting.

Until nine-year-old Alex Longstreet had come to claim the tree house, and a whole new set of dreams, as his own.

How could Jake dare to cut down this special tree, cruelly rip apart this singularly splendid tree house?

Surely there had to be another way, some way, to save them? To save the memories, the smiles, the gentle, fading images of her aunt and uncle as they had poured their energies, and their love, into creating this fairy-tale fantasyland for a displaced city child who was feeling homesick her first time away from her mommy and daddy.

Brushing tears from her eyes, her worries of today taking a back seat to the memories of yesterday, Susannah knelt down in front of a small cabinet, opening the doors to see that her china tea set still sat inside on the single shelf, each cup nestled against its matching saucer, the teapot with its chipped spout still sitting where she had left it.

It was silly, it was stupid, but she could not resist the impulse to take the small pieces out and arrange them on the table, setting four places—one for Uncle Frank, one for Aunt Bitzy, one for Susannah, and one for Clarence, her imaginary friend whom her aunt and uncle always swore they could see.

She then pulled out one of the chairs and gingerly sat down, lifting the teapot as she asked, "One lump or two, Clarence?"

"Two, and a splash of cream, if you don't mind," Jake Longstreet said as he bent himself nearly in half to enter the suddenly minuscule chamber. "And I suppose you'll be serving up a dish of crow for me to have with my tea—unless you'd care to come out onto the porch and share what I brought as a peace offering for nearly taking your head off this morning?"

Susannah blinked rapidly, trying to rid her eyes of her last sentimental tears. "I didn't hear you come up the steps," she said, unable to think of anything else to say as she lowered the teapot to the table with a shaking hand, wincing as the lid clattered, giving away her nervousness.

"I'm in training as a cat burglar," Jake said, smiling in the dim light. "Everyone should have a second career to fall back on, don't you think? After all, this lawyer stuff might not pan out."

Susannah began replacing the teacups in the cabinet, purposely keeping her back to Jake as she worked. "How did you know I was here?"

"I saw a light through the trees, and figuratively went out on a limb, I guess you'd say. After all," he added, handing her the teapot as she knelt on the rag rug, "Aunt Bitzy doesn't report until tomorrow morning."

"It is getting late, though," Susannah said, closing the doors of the cabinet and rising to her feet. She brushed the dust off her hands as she wished Jake Longstreet to the other side of the moon. "Should Alex be alone?"

"Maria's with him," he answered, then motioned for her to precede him through the doorway and back onto the porch of the tree house. "Alex and I just had a long after-dinner discussion on the perils and pitfalls associated with speaking to the press, and I think he's sulking in his bedroom."

"I'm sorry, Jake," Susannah told him sincerely as she closed the door to the tree house, shutting the door on her childhood memories once more. "I don't think he meant any harm, though."

"No, of course he didn't," Jake responded, sitting down cross-legged on the front porch of the tree house. "Neither does your Aunt Bitzy—although I've really had to work on accepting that one, I have to tell you. It's kind of like finding out that the Tooth Fairy has a dark side."

"I think she'd prefer to call it her romantic side, Jake," Susannah said, sitting down beside him, her eyes on the red-and-white checked cotton napkin covering what looked to be a picnic basket. "Aunt Bitzy really doesn't have a devious bone in her body." She looked past Emily's branches and into the rapidly falling darkness. "Well, maybe a couple. Two or three—tops."

"I blame the reporter, actually," Jake said, lifting the napkin to expose a bottle of champagne and two crystal flutes. "He had no business talking to Alex in the first place. Although I do rather like Eddie the nail biter's picture."

"It was taken from behind, Jake," Susannah protested, remembering the photograph, and cringing. "The only good thing about it was that nobody could possibly recognize me."

"Really?" he teased, working the cork out of the bottle. "I would have recognized you anywhere. Those long legs. That rather nice view of your—"

"Is that really champagne?" Susannah interrupted quickly, longing for a change of subject. "I must have had a zillion tea parties up here with Emily, but champagne was definitely not on the menu. Cocoa from a thermos, water, lemonade—but never champagne."

"It's the real stuff, Susannah. And strawberries to go with the champagne," Jake added, reaching into the basket and pulling out a sterling-silver bowl holding a half-dozen chocolate-dipped strawberries, each the size of a small lemon. "I've had these in the refrigerator for a couple of days, wondering why I bought them. Now it seems like I must have been inspired. They do make a pretty good peace offering, don't you think?"

He looked so adorably sheepish in the light from the lantern, his dark hair falling forward over his forehead, the open collar of his white dress shirt glowing in the half-light. And when he handed her a flute of bubbling champagne, Susannah knew she could forgive the man anything.

She took a sip of her drink, the champagne bubbles tickling her nose, then smiled over the top of the glass as she tilted her head to one side, looking out over the large, dark expanse that would soon be Jake Longstreet's yard.

"I used to sit up here at night and think that I was taller than the whole world—and that the whole world could be seen from this tree house," she said, almost as if she were alone, and speaking to herself out loud. "Uncle Frank called it my 'imagining place,' and it was, it truly was."

She turned to Jake, smiling, her eyes awash in dreams. "I could be anything when I was up here. An astronaut. A scientist about to make a new discovery that would entirely eliminate the need for school. A general, commanding her army. A—" She stopped, feeling herself flush in the darkness.

"A princess, waiting in her tower for her Prince Charming to come rescue her?" Jake asked quietly as he offered her a strawberry, smiling when she took a bite of the chocolate-dipped confection as he held it out to her. "Would he put you on his great white stallion, and carry you off to his castle?"

The chocolate was sweet on her tongue, the slight tartness of the strawberry sending a shiver down her spine. Or was it the teasing, seductive look in Jake's eyes that had caused the delicious frisson that momentarily tickled her, frightened her even as it delighted?

"All young girls dream of princes, Jake," she said as sternly as she could, taking another sip of champagne before carefully placing the flute on the porch floor. "And we all kissed a bunch of toads before we figured out that there ain't no such animal outside of storybooks."

"Then I guess there's no sense in applying for the job, is there?" Jake asked, popping the remainder of the strawberry into his own mouth. "Aunt Bitzy and Alex will be devastated, I suppose, but then again, who ever heard of a lawyer in the role of Prince Charming?"

Susannah laughed. "Are you guys just below or just above used-car salesmen in the ranks of the least trusted people in the world?"

"Below used-car salesmen and above politicians, I think," he answered, draining his glass and then reaching across her to set it beside hers. "Can we be honest with each other for a minute, Susannah?" he then asked, his face just inches from hers, his left hand still braced against the porch floor, so that she couldn't even breathe deeply without touching him.

"Honest?" Susannah nearly squeaked out the word, wishing she couldn't smell his after-shave, wishing he would stop breathing all the air and making her feel light-headed, wishing they had somehow met in Manhattan and not here, with this business of Emily, and nosy reporters, and wistfully manipulating aunts, and even the sweet, hopeful Alex, to muddle the thing. "I—I suppose so."

He pushed himself away from her, so that he was once more sitting beside her, the two of them staring out into the darkness, and the only sounds for long moments were those of crickets calling to their mates, and the faraway hoot of an owl.

"Jennifer took everything I had, Susannah," Jake said quietly, so that Susannah bit her lip, knowing that if she told him she could care less about his relationship with the Broadway star she would not only be lying, she might also be cutting off what could be an important conversation.

"I know nobody would believe there could be any such animal as a gullible lawyer, but you're looking at one," he went on, his hand beginning to move up and down her bare forearm, the stroking movement seeming to be unintentional, as if he was not aware he was even touching her. "Jennifer was a hell of an actress, and she had me believing she loved me. Really loved me. When I found out the truth I was nearly destroyed."

"Jake, you don't have to explain anything to me," Susannah said softly, as she could already tell where this confession was leading. "You don't believe in love anymore, and you most certainly don't believe in princesses or princes—or even happily-ever-afters. Neither do I. That's why fairy tales are for children, not adults."

"Been burned a time or two yourself, have you?" he asked, smiling at her as his entire body seemed to relax once more.

"Just once, but once was enough," Susannah admitted. "I like my life the way it is now. Neat. Orderly. Unencumbered. Oh, someday, if it happens, I'll be thrilled to fall in love again. But it will be real, grown-up love—and not the sort Disney puts to music."

"The kind Aunt Bitzy and my son believe in, you mean?" He was still stroking her arm, and once in a while his fingertips inadvertently brushed the side of her breast.

She leaned over and picked up her champagne, draining the glass. "Poor Mr. Wadlow," she said, forcing a hint of laughter into her voice. "He won't be winning any Pulitzers for follow-ups of his little story in this morning's newspaper."

"And Aunt Bitzy will have to go back to her romance novels if she wants a happy ending," Jake said, then sighed. "But it's Alex I'm worried about. I never realized how much he misses having a mother. So much so, that he's inventing fairy tales of his own."

Acting purely out of impulse, Susannah laid a hand on Jake's arm. "You're a good father, Jake," she told him honestly. "I haven't seen much of Alex, I'll admit, but what I've seen is wonderful. He's happy, well adjusted, polite—as well as adorable. And you've brought him here to Allentown, out of Manhattan, doing your best to give him a normal childhood. You have nothing to be ashamed of, you know. And this Emily thing? Hey, he'll forget it after a while. Kids are resilient that way."

"I don't know about that, Susannah," Jake answered, leaning back against the door of the tree house, his long legs pushed out in front of him across the entire width of the porch. "I saw the expression on your face when you were in here." He motioned over his shoulder with his thumb. "You looked as happy as Alex does on Christmas morning. The kid is batty about this damn tree house. How do I destroy that happiness and not scar him in some way?"

Susannah shrugged, deciding it was safer to keep the discussion centered on Emily, and not on anything remotely connected with Alex's hope, Aunt Bitzy's hope—that romance would blossom in the cradling branches of Emily the elm tree. "Perhaps you can get another opinion on Emily's health. Maybe all this furor is over nothing. After all, we're both full-size adults, and I don't hear any branches creaking to warn us that the whole tree is about to fall down at any moment."

"Did it," Jake answered her, pushing a hand through his hair, so that Susannah's palms itched to trace that same path herself. "I called in a guy from a tree service in Bethlehem. He agrees with Fred. Emily's got to go before the next winter freeze. And, before you ask, there's no way to dismantle the tree house and reassemble it in another tree. The wood's too old and weathered, for one thing, and there aren't any other suitable trees on my property."

Susannah thought about her little table and chairs, the rag rug, the pictures hanging on the walls just behind the door she and Jake were propped against, discussing an elm tree as if it were a loved one in intensive care.

"There's a line from Shakespeare," Jake said after a small silence. "Something about if something is to be done, then it is better it be done quickly. Fred will be here Thursday, Susannah. Please tell your aunt so that there won't be any scenes, all right? I can't even think about having to force her out of the tree house, with Alex beside her, glaring at me as if I'm the biggest ogre in all of fantasyland."

"Thursday? That's only four days from now," Susannah whispered, wishing she didn't feel like crying. "Oh, Jake—this is going to be awful for you. For everyone."

"I know," he said, reaching across her to pick up the flutes and replace them in the basket, alongside the uneaten strawberries. "I imagine I'll be getting hate mail from half the city. But I can't let this drag on any longer. Alex is beginning to have nightmares about men with axes."

"Oh, poor baby!" Susannah exclaimed, wondering if she felt sorrier for the father or the son. "This is all Aunt Bitzy's fault, although she doesn't know what she's done. Jake—listen—I'll explain everything to her, and then she can talk to Alex. I know my aunt, and she'd rather lose Emily than have Alex suffering any more nightmares. She'll go to the cemetery, have a long talk with Uncle Frank, and then make Alex understand that Emily has to go."

"Thanks, Susannah," Jake said, leaning over to give her a kiss on the cheek. A friendly kiss. Maybe even a brotherly kiss. Not at all the sort of kiss he had given her before. Not at all the sort of kiss she wanted from him now. "I thought I could count on you. You have all the qualities of a true princess—and you're practical, as well. Some man is going to be very lucky to find you."

"Yeah," Susannah agreed, wondering why she thought her heart might be breaking. "I'm a real prize, I am." She took a deep breath, then asked, "How are you going to handle the press if they come back looking for a follow-up to today's ridiculous story?"

"I haven't, as the British say, the foggiest notion," he told her, although this time his smile was unshadowed by worries over his son. "I only hope the story hasn't made you reconsider staying here in Allentown and decorating my new house."

"No, no, of course it hasn't," Susannah said, wishing she could tell him the truth, admitting that she would be a lot smarter to run back to New York before she knew herself to be even a heartbeat closer to falling in love with a man who had already told her he would never love again. "Unless you think it would be better for Alex if I wasn't on the scene anymore?"

"Better for Alex? Oh, I see what you mean. That princess thing, right?" He shook his head. "No, I don't think that's necessary. In fact, if he sees us together, and sees that nothing is going on between us, he'll soon find something else to occupy his mind. His day camp is having an overnight jamboree soon, this Wednesday night as a matter of fact, so he's got plenty to keep him busy.''

Nothing is going on between us. The words sent sharp needles of pain into Susannah's skin, stinging her, so that she smiled all the brighter, saying, "A purely professional arrangement, Jake. No more lapses into fantasy, right?''

"Fantasy." His hands gripped her shoulders in the darkness, the unexpected action causing her to close her eyes as a shudder ran through her body. "It wasn't all that bad, was it, Cookie?" he asked, lowering her against the weathered boards of the porch only because she made no move to stop him.

She even raised her hands to slide them around his neck, pulling him close against her as the battery of the lantern accommodatingly lost power and the light dimmed, then died. "No, Jake. It wasn't bad at all. Really."

His voice was a low growl, invading her every pore. "I agree. Even levelheaded grown-ups are occasionally allowed our moments...our flashes of fantasy...of desire...of need."

"Jake, this is crazy," she said as he began pressing kisses against her jawline, her exposed throat. "Neither of us wants this, has room for this in our lives. I— I'm just establish—establishing my business." She could barely speak, for all her breath was gone, leaving her in a rush as his hand cupped one cotton-covered breast. "And you...you and Alex are beginning a new life. You don't want to be involved. I don't want... Oh, Jake!"

9

Jake closed his eyes to what he saw in Susannah's, the questions that floated in their cool, sea green depths, the rising desire he saw there—hoped he saw there, needed to see there.

Pretend. Pretend. It was easy to pretend. Pretend he was merely attracted to her. Pretend they were two consenting adults. Pretend neither of them wanted anything more than the moment, needed anything more than the moment. Pretend that he was capable of anything more lasting than that moment.

Pretend that, when it was over, he could walk away, heart whole.

It was so easy to pretend.

Pretend Susannah wasn't the loveliest, the sweetest, the most honest person to enter his orbit in far too many years.

Pretend that this growing desire for her, evident since that first day she had come into his life quoting Ogden Nash, was merely a transitory thing, something he could handle, something he could enjoy, and then forget.

She was blond. Like Jennifer. She was beautiful. Like Jennifer.

But she wasn't Jennifer.

Jennifer had never looked at Alex in that sweet, soft-eyed way. Not in the nearly two years she had been his mother. Not in that last, long, tension-fraught year she had fought for custody, when she couldn't even remember her own son's birthday.

He was done with love. Finished. For a long time, he had been done with desire.

But not in ten long years had he felt such desire as he did now. Such longing. Such a willingness to give, such a need to take.

And it was wrong. It was so very, very wrong.

"Susannah," he breathed against her mouth, her soft, inviting mouth. "I can't make any promises. I can't even promise not to hurt you. But I want you. I don't want to want you, but I do. And I think you want me."

"Don't make me say it, Jake," she whispered, her voice husky. "Don't talk at all. You've said enough. I understand."

He kissed her then, and she kissed him back, opening to him, allowing him access to her champagne-and-strawberry sweetness.

She eased her arms away from his neck, only to slip them around his back, so that he could feel her spread fingers heating him, cradling him, holding him close in the manner of someone clutching fast to something they felt would otherwise slip away and be lost to them.

His hold on her was much the same, shaping, molding, exploring, but never leaving her body for an instant, sure that she would disappear like something out of a fairy tale.

But his desire was no figment of his imagination. He couldn't get enough of her mouth, enough of the feel of her, the taste of her. He drank from her willing ardor as a man dying of thirst took sustenance from a pitcher of cool water—wanting to take all of her at once, yet knowing that it would be best to go slowly.

Somehow, her ivory breasts became bare in the moonlight that filtered through the tree branches, revealing a glory to him that he committed to memory with his eyes, his hands, his mouth.

The flare of her hip burned against him as he divested himself of his own clothing, then quickly pressed his body against her once more, afraid she might otherwise vanish into the night, disappear into the nebulous world of dreams unfulfilled, of passions lost and never regained.

Susannah was not a passive lover, accepting but not giving, taking but not offering, more concerned with not mussing her hair than surrendering to the moment. Not Susannah. She was his partner in this impetuous, yet long-dreamed-of interlude among the treetops.

Her kiss was alternately sweet and passionate; her hands first glided, then gripped fiercely. And the soft moans that barely escaped her long throat as he slid into her soft heat nearly caused his brain to explode.

They were no longer in the tree house. They were floating, high among the summer stars, looking down at the world through eyes that might be closed, but could see forever.

He was buried in her...reborn in her...lost in her...found in her.

And when it was over, when all the starbursts and rockets of their private fireworks display had drifted toward earth once more, their brilliant, fast-burning light slowly dying as it neared the ground, he was in awe of her.

For she knew he wanted nothing to do with love, with happily-ever-after. And now, now that it was over, and they were both quietly, separately, dressing themselves once more in the clothing that declared them two people rather than the single entity their lovemaking had temporarily made them, she seemed neither furtive, nor shamed, nor sorry.

He had asked. She had given. They both had shared.

It was so wrong. It was so right.

And it was a beginning, if he wanted it. If he dared to place his once-shattered faith in fairy tales, in happy endings.

"Are you all right?" Jake asked at last, the full moon making it possible for him to watch as Susannah pushed her hands through her hair, its sleek curtain of blond glory obligingly going back into place around the smooth oval of her face. "These old boards aren't exactly soft."

"I'm fine, really," she answered, closing the last two buttons of her blouse. "Emily might not be entirely sound, but the tree house still seems sturdy enough. You know, Jake, of all the dreams I've had up here, I have to tell you, making love in a tree house was never one of my fantasies. I'll never look at this place the same way again."

"I can understand that," he said, taking her hand to help her to the curving stairs, so that they could descend to the deeper darkness on the ground. "Fairytale-princess stories are more the 'fade to black' sort of romances, aren't they?"

He stopped just at the bottom of the steps, keeping Susannah on the step above him, allowed the basket to drop to the grass, and looked levelly into her eyes. "I didn't plan this, you know. It just happened, although it's entirely my fault. Are you sorry, Cookie?" he asked, not realizing that he had just turned a childhood nickname into a term of endearment.

She shook her head. "No, Jake. I'm not sorry. Are you?"

"Not right now, no," he answered truthfully, smiling at her in the darkness. "But I can't make any promises about tomorrow. I guess the only thing I can't be sure of is how I'll feel tomorrow. God knows, I don't feel now the way I did an hour ago. As a matter of fact, remembering what I said about never falling in love again, I think I was being a pompous ass an hour ago."

"If you're expecting an argument from me, Jake, please don't hold your breath," Susannah said, lightly stepping past him to the well-worn path leading to Aunt Bitzy's back porch, where a light burned in the darkness.

He maneuvered himself in front of her, pulled her close against him, slipping his arms around her waist as she rested her hands on his shoulders. "What?" she asked, the smile on her face making him grin in return.

"Nothing earthshaking, Cookie. Just give me some time, okay? My nearly decade-old ideas about a well-ordered life have gone straight to hell in the last few days, and I'm still fighting the feeling that Aunt Bitzy has slipped some sort of potion into my chocolate-chip cookies."

"Do you think you're falling under the Good Witch Bitzy's spell, Jake?" Susannah asked, reaching up to kiss a corner of his mouth. "That doesn't say much for my feminine allure, does it? Or do you think I'm under a spell, too?"

"I don't know. Maybe we're both unknowingly acting out your aunt's idea of a romance novel—although I doubt she would have approved of her niece appearing in this latest scene," he answered, kissing her quickly—quickly, so that he would be able to let her go. "All I know right now is that I want you to stay here, in Allentown. I don't want to lose you before I know for sure what I may have found."

"I'll think about it, Jake," Susannah said quietly. "You know, you do have this way of arranging things as they suit you. A steak instead of the salad I wanted, telling me what I want because you think I might want it. Just don't think I made love with you tonight only because you wanted it. I'm a big girl now, and I make my own decisions, and perform my own first aid if I fall and scrape my knees—or bruise my heart. And if I do decide to stay, even if I decide that I'm in love with you, it will be my decision. What you do, is yours."

He let her go then, knowing he could not hold her any longer. He had to go home, let Maria go to her room, check on his sleeping son—and think.

Had enough time passed? he wondered as he watched Maria march across the yard to her apartment over the garage of the rented house.

He closed the door and locked it, walking slowly through the rented house, turning off lights as he made his way to the stairs.

Had the hole in his heart healed sufficiently for him to think of opening it to possible injury, possible happiness, once more?

Did Alex really need a mother? he questioned silently as he looked in on his sleeping son.

Did he really need a wife? he asked just as silently as he opened the door to his own room and stared at the wide, empty bed.

They had been doing just fine, just the two of them, for a lot of years now.

The wounds had healed, the scars had lost their angry red hue, and they were making a new beginning, away from Manhattan, away from the memories that had faded but could be brought into sharp focus once more with a single local headline recounting the custody battle that had nearly destroyed them.

Did they really need to allow another woman into their lives?

Most important, after Jennifer, could he really trust his heart, his judgment again? This was all happening so quickly, so without warning—just the way he had met, and then married, Jennifer within a short, wildly wonderful month.

But Susannah wasn't Jennifer. She never would be, could be, Jennifer.

All right. So, what was she?

She's a chance you might never have again, a small, quiet voice whispered inside his head as he sat on the edge of the bed and turned out the light.

"You've got a rather satisfied-cat-who-just-ate-the-canary smirk on your face this morning, young lady," Aunt Bitzy said as she set a plate of French toast in front of Susannah.

"Do I, Aunt Bitzy?" Susannah asked, reaching for the pot of honey. "I was just thinking about something I learned in high school. Something some Roman said. Now, how did it go?" She slowly drizzled some sweet, golden honey in a widening circle on the French toast. A golden circle, just like a wedding ring. "Oh, yes—'I came, I saw, I conquered'—that was it. A lovely saying, don't you think, Aunt Bitzy?"

"That would depend, Cookie," her aunt supplied as she sat down across from her at the table, lifting her coffee cup and looking at her niece over the brim. "The quote you refer to is from Suetonius in *Lives of the Caesars*. It was Julius who supposedly said the words—*Veni, vidi, vici*. Are you feeling somewhat warlike this morning, dear? Because you don't look it in the least. You look rather dreamy—my favorite author, Araminta Raven, would have said your eyes were starlike, filled with the sublime joy and wonder of incandescent love."

"Oh, yeah?" Susannah said, grinning so widely that she could feel the skin of her cheeks stretching. "I think I've got to read that lady's work. Isn't it a beautiful morning, Aunt Bitzy?"

"Lovely, dear, lovely—but please don't change the subject. As your aunt, and as a woman who is particularly astute in matters of the heart, if I may say so, I believe I should like to hear more about whatever has caused this glow in my only niece. You were out rather late last night, I do believe. I tried to stay up, but this having to be with Emily at seven each morning does not allow me to burn much midnight oil, you understand."

"Sorry, Aunt Bitzy," Susannah said, surprised to see that she had already finished off half her French toast. She hadn't known being in love could make her so hungry. "You're just going to have to wait for the book to come out to read the ending. But there is something we have to discuss," she ended, losing her smile at last.

"Oh, pooh!" Aunt Bitzy said, although she didn't seem to be too distressed. "All right. I'll wait until you're ready to talk to me. But remember this, missy— you've never kept a secret from me in all your life. And, as I do recall seeing that determined look in your eye a time or two before this morning, I have no fears as to how everything will work out. You set your sights on something, and you go get it. I think you get that from your Uncle Frank. He told me he knew the night he first saw me that I was the one for him, and he didn't give up until I agreed to marry him. I do adore masterful men, don't you?"

Susannah fiddled with her teaspoon, waiting for her aunt to stop to take a breath, which didn't happen for several more minutes, as she was telling her niece, not for the first time, exactly where and how Uncle Frank had proposed.

Keeping an interested look on her face, Susannah retreated inside her own mind, reliving yet again that incredible moment when she had realized that she was in love with Jake Longstreet.

It had been just before he'd kissed her...just after he'd so earnestly told her he couldn't make her any promises...and precisely at that instant when she had known that it didn't matter whether or not he thought he loved her, because he did love her. He had to love her.

Now all she had to do was to wait, patiently, while the man figured it out for himself. It was that simple. And hang Jennifer Merchant and her alley-cat morals. Susannah Yardley would never stray from her husband. Not in a million years. He'd figure that out, too. She'd make sure of it!

Veni, vidi, vici. Maybe she'd have those words carved into a bust of Julius Caesar and they could keep it in the library of the new house....

"Aunt Bitzy," Susannah interrupted just as her aunt began telling of her honeymoon in Niagara Falls, snapping both her aunt and herself back to reality. "There isn't much time before you have to go sit with Emily, so I have to tell you something. Something about Alex—and Emily. And about nightmares. Please listen carefully."

"And so, dear Alex, now that I've decided that Fred is right, the time has come to say goodbye to Emily. Not that she'll ever be far from our hearts, for we'll always have our memories of our time in the tree house, won't we?"

"I guess so," Alex said, his chin quivering, but only slightly, his innocent-angel eyes tear-bright, but unblinking. "Are you going to be all right, Aunt Bitzy?" he asked, his unselfish concern for her aunt nearly breaking Susannah's heart.

"Oh, darling boy," Aunt Bitzy exclaimed, hugging the child close against her soft bosom, a comfort zone Susannah could still remember from her own childhood. "Of course, I'll be all right. And we still have two whole days to spend with Emily—isn't that right, Jake?"

Susannah looked to Jake across the table on the patio of his rented house, loving him for the sadness he wasn't afraid to show in his own eyes.

"Two whole days, Alex," he promised gravely. "But then you go back to camp. Remember—you have a sleep-over Wednesday night." The sound of a car horn beeping in front of the house was followed by Jake's rising to his feet. "Now, please excuse me while I go out front and tell the driver you won't be going to camp either today or tomorrow. And champ," he added, his voice soft and vulnerable, "thanks for understanding, okay? And thank you, Aunt Bitzy. You're a marvel, a real marvel."

Alex and Aunt Bitzy went off toward the tree house, hand in hand, leaving Susannah alone to wipe at her tear-filled eyes without fear of discovery before Jake returned to the backyard and took up his seat at the table once more.

He looked relieved that the siege of Emily and the tree house had come to an end, but there was a cautious, almost-embarrassed look in his eyes that told Susannah that the events of the prior evening were still very much on his mind.

Not that his next words proved her right.

"I phoned Cynthia early last evening and explained that you won't be available to work on her condo until the end of August," he said matter-of-factly as he poured himself another cup of coffee. "She was very agreeable, although she mentioned something about now wanting you to do some rooms at her summer cottage, as well. Some cottage. I think the damn place covers an acre, not counting the gardens and beachfront. Anyway, when she figured out that I wanted you, she said, and I quote: 'I must have her, Jake. I simply must!'"

He winked at Susannah, not seeing that she had drawn her hands into tight fists beneath the table. "I'm thinking of asking for a discount now that I've done so much to help boost your career. Hey, smile, Cookie—I'm kidding! But this is great news, I think. Cindy will be touting your name to her entire circle—and it's a very wide, extremely well-heeled circle."

"Really," Susannah said, not trusting her voice to say more.

"Uh-hmm," Jake mumbled as he took a sip of coffee, still oblivious to Susannah's sudden homicidal tendencies. "But don't let it go to your head. That group would hang moss from the walls if it was the 'in' thing to do. Just go get 'em while they're hot, and you'll have a dozen or more juicy commissions before Labor Day."

"Well, whoop-de-do," Susannah ground out, replacing her cup on its saucer with enough impact to shake the table. "And I suppose, in lieu of that discount you mentioned, you'd just make do with a fulsome thank-you. Hey—and maybe another quick roll in the hay? Well, you can just hold your breath waiting for that, Jake Longstreet, because it ain't gonna happen!''

He put down his own coffee cup and smiled—how dare he smile at her! "You do jump to conclusions, don't you, Susannah?" he said more than asked, rising to come around the table and stand behind her chair, so that she had no choice but to allow him to help her rise.

She was instantly embarrassed, and just as quickly contrite. Of course, Jake wasn't the sort to demand sexual favors. If she knew nothing else about him, she knew that. But that didn't mean she wasn't still angry. Damn angry.

Wheeling about to glare at him, and without apologizing for what she had said, she declared, "You had no right to call Mrs. Thorogood, Jake. No right at all. I'm a big girl now. I've been free-lancing for over a year, and I make and pay my own way. And I most certainly don't need you to run interference for me."

"I did it again, didn't I?" Jake questioned her, scratching at a spot just behind his left ear. "Made another decision for you. And after you told me last night that you'd make up your own mind as to whether or not you'll stay here in Allentown for a while. You know, my last law assistant told me I didn't know how to delegate authority—always wanting to do everything myself."

She followed him as he walked along the brick path that led to the front of the house. "You could use some work in that area," she told him, allowing him to take her hand and raise it to his lips—a sweet, courtly gesture that would have had Aunt Bitzy applauding his romantic expertise.

"Maybe we could figure out some sort of password," he said, opening the passenger door of his car and motioning for her to seat herself. "Then, every time I start taking charge of things I could just as easily leave to the person concerned, you could shout it out and I'd know I should back off."

"Geronimo!" Susannah stated firmly, planting her feet on the driveway and crossing her arms over her waist.

"Yes," Jake answered, nodding. "Geronimo would be a good word, I suppose. We've got a nine o'clock appointment to go through my furniture at the warehouse, so we'd better hurry."

Susannah laughed, shaking her head. "You still don't get it, do you, Jake? I said, *Geronimo*. As in, hey, guess what, you didn't ask me if I could go to the warehouse this morning. You just led me to the car and *expected* me to go with you."

He closed the car door and leaned his long frame against it. "I did say we'd go to the warehouse, didn't I?"

"You did. And I said I'd go with you. I just didn't say precisely *when* I'd go with you," Susannah told him, amazed at how much she loved this man when he was looking sheepish. And she didn't really want to change him. She simply wanted him to know that she had a will of her own. "You just picked up the ball and started running with it."

"Ouch!" Jake shook his head, wincing at her description of his actions. Then, quickly employing the smile that had the power to turn Susannah's knees to jelly, he said, "Would it be all right if we took a ride over to the warehouse to see my furniture this morning? If you're busy, I'm sure we can arrange the visit for any time that is convenient to you, Ms. Yardley. I await your decision."

"Nut!" Susannah exclaimed, playfully pushing him to one side so that she could pull open the car door and slip inside, then looked up at him. "So? What are you waiting for? I want to see that grand piano!"

10

The warehouse wasn't air-conditioned and the heat in the high-ceilinged building was stifling, not that Susannah seemed to notice.

She was like a child on a treasure hunt, peeking under covers, opening boxes, ooh-ing and ah-ing as she delighted in each new discovery.

And there were plenty of discoveries to make, as Jake had accumulated a lot of furniture over the years, much of it his own, much of it belonging to his parents. There were valuable prints, original oils from his grandfather's extensive collection, mirrors of every shape and size.

The large, intricately designed metal four-poster bed frame seemed to particularly delight Susannah, who nodded enthusiastically when he explained that it had belonged to his parents, and that his mother had always draped the antique gunmetal gray frame with white organdy for the summer and a green and a blue tapestry during the winter months.

''The bed was part of their furniture in the family home,'' he had told her as she located the boxes holding the bed drapes and even matching draperies. "I've never slept in the thing, myself," he'd added quietly, wanting her to understand that this bed had not been a part of his brief marriage to Jennifer. That seemed important to him. He had hoped it might be important to Susannah, as well.

He sat on an overturned crate and watched in mingled amusement and amazement as Susannah matched side chairs to tables, cabinets to bedsteads—tucking pertinent facts about each piece of furniture into some sort of mental filing cabinet, then pulling out the correct piece when she discovered one that was companionable to it.

She was in her element in this warehouse, surrounded by all the boxes and cartons, her blond hair slipping free of a no-nonsense ponytail she had twisted it into when they first entered the building, the smudges of dust on her face not detracting at all from her fresh, vibrant beauty.

And she didn't care that it was hot, or that she was getting dirty, or that she had scraped open one knuckle on the edge of a crate, or that Jake was just sitting and watching while she wrestled with a padded cover, trying to replace it over the antique inlaid-rosewood dining table whose beauty had nearly reduced her to tears.

"Mr. Longstreet? You gonna be much longer? Not that I'm tryin' to rush you or anything, but's time for my lunch break, you understand, and I—"

"If you leave me the key, George, we'll lock up when we go, if that's all right," Jake volunteered, grinning as Susannah gave the quilted cover a mighty shake, then sneezed at the cloud of dust the action had sent flying into the air.

"I really shouldn't," the custodian began, then grinned. "Aw, what the heck. Most everything in here belongs to you, anyway. Here you go," he said, handing Jake a large ring of keys. "Use the big silver one, and then drop the whole bunch at the main gate. I'll pick 'em up there."

"Thank you, George," Jake said, then immediately forgot him as he heard Susannah exclaim from somewhere out of sight of him, "Oh, how beautiful! Jake? Jake—come here. You've got to see this!"

He followed the sound of her voice, quickly locating her behind a tall stack of packing boxes, all of them bearing the name Longstreet. She was sitting cross-legged on the dusty concrete floor, staring at the bronze bust of Beethoven she held cradled in her lap, almost as if she were holding a child. "Your grandmother kept this on the piano, didn't she?" she asked, not looking at him. "I know it's almost a cliché to plop good old Ludwig there, but this bust is so beautifully made, I can't resist it."

"As long as you also put the tapestry drape on top," Jake told her, going down on his haunches beside her and reaching into the foam-pellet-filled box, pulling out the fringed tapestry a moment later. "It's so long that I used to hide under it when I was a kid, and pretend nobody could see me."

"Oh, really?" Susannah responded, grinning. "And here I thought you were born all grown-up and already a lawyer. Unfold it, Jake, so I can see the colors. This may be just what I was looking for to set the color scheme in the great room."

"Great room?" Jake repeated as he began unfolding the tapestry. "Is that the latest interior-decorator name for a family room?"

"It could be, and so politically correct, too. But you have to admit it, Jake, it's a *great* room. Oh! What a beautiful piece! Burgundy, navy, cream—everything I could see when I first envisioned the room. I want to take that with me today, as well as a few of the draperies and a flower vase I found a while ago. For the colors, you understand."

She looked at him, her eyes sparkling. "Your house is nearly going to decorate itself, Jake. All I have to do is pick the right paints and papers that will pull it all together."

"Then I am going to be eligible for some sort of discount," Jake said, helping her to her feet after she carefully repacked the bust.

"In your dreams, buster," Susannah replied, brushing at the front of her blouse and slacks, doing very little to dislodge the dust that had settled onto her clothing. She grinned up at him. "But I will give you full points for effort."

"Agreed. And I'll give you lunch, once we go home and clean up. But first, I want to show you something you missed." He took her hand and led her farther down the aisle between two stacks of his furnishings, stopping when they got to the end of the aisle and the single quilted packing-blanket-covered piece.

"This is my pride and joy, Susannah," he said, laying his palms on the blanket. "I want it to go in my study, all right? And it goes in just the way it is. No improvements."

She looked at him quizzically. "It's a desk, by the looks of it. Of course, Jake. If you want it in the study—hey, it goes in the study. Everything you own is magnificent, and I imagine the desk is, as well. May I see it now? Or maybe you're waiting for the drum-roll?"

Watch her face, Jake told himself as he grasped the packing blanket in his hands. *Watch her eyes. Eyes don't lie.*

He gave the cover a tug and the huge rolltop desk was revealed in all its ugliness. It was oak, for one thing, so that the wood matched nothing else in the large inventory of cherry and mahogany Longstreet furniture.

But that wasn't enough to make it ugly, for oak was not ugly. However, leaving to one side the fact that the sliding wood cover that made it a rolltop desk was missing, the piece was battered and bruised, the victim of fifty years of hard use by a man who had often slept with his head on the desk top and eaten many of his meals there, as well.

Two of the drawer pulls didn't match the originals, there were half-a-dozen burn scars from a cigar left burning too long as it perched on the edge of the desk top, and—although Susannah couldn't know it—the lock on the middle drawer hadn't worked since Jake had met Professor Allerson some twenty years previously.

Jake didn't realize he was holding his breath until it came out in a rush as Susannah touched the desk top and said, "Someone very special to you owned this desk, didn't they, Jake?"

"One of my law professors," he said, pulling the cover back over the desk once more before turning to look at her. "Old Man Allerson, we called him. He spent half his life teaching, all the time doing pro bono work on the side. He was brilliant, Susannah. Really brilliant. He could have been rich, but he wanted to teach. And to help people. I adored the man."

"And he gave you his desk?"

Jake nodded. "That, and his lawbooks. He died a few years ago, and those books and this desk were almost his entire estate. I had worked for him during the summers during law school. He never discouraged me from going into the area of the law I chose, saying the rich deserved to be represented as well as the poor— and might even need more protection because of the trouble they seem to get themselves into—but he made sure I'd never forget my responsibility to the law. I still do pro bono in Manhattan, and hope to do some here in Allentown. It keeps me from getting in a rut, I suppose."

"Don't go modest on me now, Jake. And the desk goes into your study as is. I promise," Susannah said as she slipped her arms around his waist and laid her head against his chest. "You do know you're making me like you more and more each time you reveal more of the real Jake, don't you, Attorney Longstreet? Quite frankly, I don't think you're playing fair."

He put his hands on her shoulders, hoping she didn't notice that his hands were trembling. What was the matter with him? He wasn't a schoolboy. And how had this woman's opinion come to mean so much to him? "Even now that I'm going to have Fred chop Emily down Thursday morning?" he joked quickly, hoping to cover his nervousness.

Susannah looked up into his face, her smile making him forget where they were, and the fact that George would be coming back from lunch at any time. "We'll still have our memories, Jake. Isn't that what Aunt Bitzy said?"

"Oh, lady," he countered gruffly, shaking his head, "you're something else. You're really something else." And then, because he couldn't help himself, and thinking wasn't exactly what he wanted to be doing at the moment, he bent his head and kissed her.

The passion he had experienced upon kissing her last night, loving her last night, came back in a blinding flash. He was instantly hungry for the taste of her, the feel of her, the sweet, giving, beauty of her.

Which is why he broke off the kiss, reluctantly letting her go and fishing in his pocket for George's keys.

"We'd better get out of here before they start charging us rent," he said, not looking at her. "That is, if you're done?"

Her expression was so loving, so very understanding, that he was almost angry with her, which was about as juvenile a reaction as he had felt in decades.

"Just help me with the tapestry and the rest of it, all right?" Susannah said, motioning to the small pile of treasures she wanted to take with her. "Lord, I didn't realize how hot and dusty it is in here. I get so carried away at the beginning of a new project. You should have stopped me an hour ago, Jake. You must be melting."

He picked up the bundle and motioned for her to precede him to the door. "Not melting, Susannah," he said quietly. "The correct word, I think, is *thawing*. Now, come on. Maria probably has lunch ready by now, and I'm suddenly starving."

He isn't going to talk about it, Susannah decided, smiling up at Maria as the housekeeper removed the empty sandwich plate from in front of her as she and Jake sat at the outdoor table. *It's been hours and hours, and he hasn't come within miles of the subject. He isn't exactly pretending last night didn't happen—which would kill me—but he isn't about to hold any postmortems, either. Maybe that's good.*

She wondered why she didn't feel more uncomfortable around him after their spontaneous intimacy; why she still felt so secure in her belief that she had not given herself to a man without any thought but the pleasure of the moment.

She was going to marry this man. It was that simple, and that complicated. She was going to marry him, be his wife forever and forever, love his son, love the children she hoped they'd have. All the lovely fairy-tale dreams her Aunt Bitzy believed in so fervently were soon to become Susannah Yardley's reality.

She believed that.

She just didn't know *why* she believed that.

But if they lived in Jake's gorgeous house, or they huddled together in a tent in the woods, she was going to be by his side. Through the good times. Through the bad times. Through every cliché in the book.

Because she loved Jake Longstreet. Loved his smile, his frowns, his sense of humor, his temper, his of-course-you-want-to-do-it-my-way attitude, his loyalty to his old professor, his love for his child. In fact, if love were a Chinese restaurant menu, and she could take two lovable traits from Column A and three from Column B, she couldn't have selected anyone who suited her so well.

"Susannah?"

She blinked, shaking her head as she snapped out of her private thoughts, suddenly aware that she had been silent ever since Maria had cleared the table. "Sorry, I was just thinking about your bedroom," she improvised wildly, then winced when she realized what she had just said. "About—about the color scheme, I mean."

He shot her that wicked, knowing, Pierce Brosnan smile, and her insides turned to butter. No, he wasn't going to talk about last night. He didn't have to. All he had to do was look at her. "Of course, Susannah. The color scheme. I sensed that immediately."

"Oh, shut up!" she exclaimed, rising from the table and rapidly heading across the lawn, toward the new house, Jake following after her, as she'd hoped he would.

Susannah remembered her manners well enough to smile and wave to two workmen who were sitting on the edge of the patio, taking their lunch break, then entered the house through the French doors, turning left and heading for the back staircase leading to the second floor.

"I know the ceramic tile in the bath and dressing area is light beige, but I want to see if it's a rosy beige or a yellow beige," she told Jake, throwing the words back to him over her shoulder as he mounted the stairs behind her.

"Yes," he said, his voice too close, "I can see where that would be highly important. At least I guess so. Do you remember the bathtub from our first visit? Alex says two people should be able to fit into it easily."

There he went again—saying things without really saying things. Or was he? What was wrong with her? One moment she was thinking he was the greatest thing since sliced bread, and the next she was longing to smack him in the mouth. Why was she suddenly so angry, so ready to pick apart anything he said? If this was what love did to a person, she'd take baloney, thank you anyway!

Either way, Susannah could feel her temper getting the better of her. She took only two more steps before she stopped short just at the entrance to the large dressing area of the master bedroom and wheeled about to face Jake. "That's not funny," she informed him, knowing she was blushing and hating her fair skin for betraying her.

"What?" he asked, spreading his arms as if he was a totally innocent man, unjustly accused. "I didn't say anything."

She opened her mouth to answer him, then mentally reviewed what he had said—and what he hadn't said, suddenly understanding that that was precisely what had destroyed her mood. "No," she admitted, shaking her head. "You didn't say anything. Not *really.* You've been polite and civil and friendly all day, as a matter of fact, and I'm only overreacting like some knee-jerk idiot. And you know what, Jake Longstreet? For all my good intentions to the contrary, I'd really like to punch you in the nose for *not* saying anything!"

"Not as mature and civilized as you thought you were, is that it, Cookie?" Jake asked, taking her hand and leading her to the deep window seat that overlooked the front of the house. "Well, welcome to the club. And you know what? I'm damn glad you don't have the etiquette for the morning-after down pat."

"Neither do you, you know," she replied, slightly mollified, yet still avoiding his eyes as she sat down.

"No, I don't. And, contrary to popular opinion, all men don't have *needs,* or bed women because they *have* to. As a matter of fact, there are even some of us who believe lovemaking is just that—being together with someone you love."

"Which means that you—" She looked at him for an instant as if he were about to declare his undying adoration of her, then slid her eyes away once more. "That you were faithful to your wife, and were absolutely crushed when you found out she—"

"Slept with anything in pants?" he ended for her. "Yes, I guess you could say it bothered me. Bothered me enough that I took Alex and the two of us sort of retired from life for a while."

She felt his hand on her forearm and turned to look at him once more, wishing she didn't want so badly to hear that he hadn't spent the last few years running from woman to woman, loving them and leaving them.

"You don't owe me any explanations, Jake," she said, saying the words because those were the words she imagined people were supposed to say in situations like this, even if people didn't mean them. "I'm a big girl now. There were two consenting adults in the tree house last night, and . . ."

Her voice trailed off, because she couldn't think of anything else to say. Nothing that was smart and sophisticated, and would lead him to believe she hadn't given him her heart as well as her body last night, hoping for his heart in return.

"Susannah?" Jake questioned her, employing the tip of his index finger beneath her chin to lift her face to his. "You don't have to say anything. We don't have to play games. Last night you gave me a gift I'll treasure forever. I'm saying this rather late, but let's go slow on this, all right? Before we say anything else, do anything else, let's be certain. All right?"

She bit her lip as she nodded her agreement, knowing that he was right again, darn him. Just because she knew she was in love with him, would always love him, that didn't mean even someone as romantically inclined as Aunt Bitzy would have expected the guy to go down on one knee and propose after a single, mind-blowing night together.

"Of course," Jake continued, grinning, "that doesn't mean I'm not going to kiss you any time you look like you do now—all misty-eyed and sad."

"In that case, I'll never smile again," Susannah retorted, deliberately pulling a comically hangdog face as she maneuvered herself within kissing distance of his intriguing mouth.

"Oh, Cookie, you're so good for me," Jake said on a sigh, just before he slanted his lips against hers, at the same time taking her fully into his arms, so that their bodies were melded together from chest to knee.

Susannah could feel her breasts tingling as she reveled in his embrace, her entire body turning hot as their kiss deepened.

"Mr. Jake, one of those nosy reporters is down— *Whoops!*"

Susannah buried her face against Jake's chest, giggling as he whispered, "The damn rules keep changing, Cookie. I thought you were the only one who could shout Geronimo."

"I'm sorry, Mr. Jake," Maria was gushing as she stood half in and half out of the bedroom doorway, wringing her hands and looking less like a retired army officer than she did a blushing young girl of sixteen. "I would have knocked, if there were any doors in this house yet, but there aren't."

"That's all right, Maria," Jake told her as he helped Susannah to rise from the window seat. "You said a reporter is here? Did he give you a card?"

The housekeeper nodded. "Not that I needed it to know who he is. He's the one from the Allentown paper. Lousy posture. Give him to me for six weeks of basic, and I'd get rid of that slouch. Should I hand him his marching papers?"

"If you can't order him in front of a firing squad, I guess I'll just have to see him," Jake said fatalistically, taking Susannah's hand and giving it a quick squeeze. "Come with me, oh, Princess of the Tree House. It's time we break the news to the press that Emily's coming down. Then maybe we can have some peace and quiet around here."

"The end of my stint as a princess? Ah, gee, and just when I was beginning to enjoy the role," Susannah replied as Jake bowed and motioned for her to precede him into the hallway, her strangely fluctuating mood on a definite upswing once more.

11

Jake and Susannah returned to the Reflections of Life restaurant Monday night for dinner, spending a lovely, lazy two hours together over good food before Jake had to go home to keep a promise to Alex concerning something to do with a computer video game.

He walked her to the front door just as the street-lights began going on along the street, pointing out that she should kiss him for getting her home before dark, and saving her from having to write another essay for her schoolteacher aunt.

Susannah complied most happily, which led to another kiss, this one initiated by Jake, and then a third, one that seemed to serve as a warning for them to say good-night to each other before it became impossible to say anything at all.

He got halfway to his car before he turned back up the brick path and kissed her again, then shook his head, chuckling ruefully as he said good-night for the second time.

Susannah stood with her hand on the doorknob, watching Jake as he opened his car door, then sprinted back up the walk a second time, rather obvious in his reluctance to leave her. He took her in his arms for another kiss, and then another, their lips clinging between these short, fervent kisses, their mingled breathing quick and hot.

"Good night, Cookie," he whispered against her throat as he held her tightly against him. "And this time I mean it. I swear it!"

"I won't hold you to that if you change your mind," Susannah told him, her hands cupping his shoulders as she pushed him away while longing to pull him close. "But Alex is waiting, isn't he?"

Jake nodded, his dark eyes shining in a way that made her feel suddenly powerful, as if she had an effect on the man he saw no need to hide. "Have breakfast with me tomorrow?" he asked, although it sounded more like an order. An order she had every intention of following to the letter.

"That's a deal, Jake. And Maria can skip the gold plate. I'll settle for the silver."

Jake laughed, kissed her on the tip of her nose, and was gone. She watched until the car's taillights disappeared around the corner, then entered the house, wondering if her aunt would notice that her feet barely touched the floor as she walked into the kitchen.

"I'm beginning to worry about how things are going with Jake, Cookie," Aunt Bitzy said without preamble as she sat at the kitchen table, a bowl of chocolate-chip cookie batter at her elbow as she waited for the latest batch to bake.

Susannah leaned over Aunt Bitzy's shoulder and stuck a finger into the batter, winning herself both a satisfying glob of the sugary stuff and a sharp slap on her wrist from her aunt who reminded her that there were raw eggs in the batter.

"Worry, Aunt Bitzy?" she asked, licking her finger and then sighing with pleasure, just as she had done since she was a child and learned to enjoy the batter almost as much as she did the finished project. "Why?"

"Because you're getting along so well, of course. Because there's no conflict in your relationship," her aunt explained in her usual rational tone as she slid an oven mitt on her right hand and answered the summons of the oven timer as it warned that the cookies were ready.

"Conflict?" Susannah repeated, remembering she had heard the word before. "Does this have anything to do with those romance novels you love so much?"

"It most certainly does, and they're right! You've made great strides in making the man notice you, but things seem stagnant now. You need some sort of conflict to get things moving again, before he gets too comfortable with the status quo. Why, if you two were getting along any better I'd be falling asleep watching you. You're boring, Cookie, *boring*."

Susannah tried to hide her smile, but failed. Personally, she believed the shooting-stars and exploding-fireworks side of her relationship with Jake was anything but boring—but of course her aunt didn't know about that, and Susannah wasn't going to tell her. "Well, I'm sorry I'm such a disappointment to you, Aunt Bitzy."

"And well you should be! It's a shame there are no pirates to kidnap you or greedy cousins out to murder Jake for his title. Then he could rescue you or you could save his life, and we could get to the happily-ever-after part. But not you two. You just smile at each other and go out to dinner—and come home before dark, for pity's sake! Without some sort of conflict to liven things up a bit, you may just go on this way for-ever and ever—and never really get anywhere."

She tested one of the cookies by pressing on it with a wooden spoon, tapping at it three times as she re-peated, "Boring, boring, *boring.*"

Susannah rescued the abused cookie from the tray, flipping it from hand to hand to try to coax the heat out of it as she sat down at the table, eager for the taste of warm, soft chocolate and well-blended brown sugar.

"I guess I see your point, Aunt Bitzy," she said ab-sently, biting into the cookie, closing her eyes as the delicious flavors mingled on her tongue. Everything seemed different to her since meeting Jake. Better. Tastes were richer, lights brighter, grass greener. It was as if he had awakened senses inside her that had been dormant all these years. "So, does that mean you're volunteering to kidnap me? You could stow me away in the tree house and hold me for ransom. What am I worth in gold doubloons, do you think?"

"Don't be facetious, young lady," Aunt Bitzy snapped, her tone warning Susannah that the woman was being deadly serious. "I know you think there's no longer any reason to hurry the thing now that Emily is being sacrificed, but opportunity only knocks once. You have him interested now, as well he should be, but it's best to strike while the iron is hot. Don't let him get comfortable with the status quo. He has to realize that what is here today may be gone tomorrow."

"A bird in the hand is worth two in the bush, and a stitch in time saves nine," Susannah quipped, adding a few more clichés as she reached for another warm cookie. "You're a riot, Aunt Bitzy, do you know that? And," she added, winking up at her aunt, "I love you very, very much."

"So you'll consider my plan to shake things up a bit?" Aunt Bitzy asked, her timeworn face alight with mischief.

"Your *plan?*" Susannah repeated, a piece of cookie lodging momentarily somewhere between her mouth and her stomach. "Lord help me, the woman has another plan! Aunt Bitzy, you're not thinking of reneging on your promise to vacate Emily Thursday morning, are you, just to get a rise out of Jake? Because that wouldn't be fair, not with Alex so worried that he—"

"Susannah Yardley, how dare you think anything so evil!" her aunt interrupted, waving the wooden spoon in her niece's direction. "I said *conflict,* not confrontation. And to use a child? Don't even think such a thing.''

Susannah went to her aunt and put her arms around her, apologizing for having thought, even for a moment, that the dear lady held so much as one malicious bone in her body. "You're an angel, Aunt Bitzy, really.''

"So your uncle Frank said, at least a million times," Aunt Bitzy said, smoothing down her apron once Susannah returned to her chair. "And now—for my plan. It seems that Matilda Mathewson, my neighbor three doors down on the right, has her grandson visiting her from Virginia this week. He's a doctor—a veterinarian, actually, but who's quibbling, as he still gets to use the word *doctor* in front of his name, which can't help but impress people. Anyway, Donald—that's his name, Donald—is a lovely man, about Jake's age, and single. Matilda's arthritis is acting up, so that she worries that Donald is bored because she can't get out and show him the sights, so I thought—''

"Forget it!" Susannah all but shouted, jumping up from her seat and heading out of the kitchen. "I will not play games, Aunt Bitzy, no matter how much you think Jake and I need conflict to move our association to some other stage—or whatever the heck you believe making him jealous would do. It's only been a a few days, for crying out loud, and I think things have been moving plenty fast enough, if you want my opinion.''

She stopped at the archway, just beneath the four-leaf-clover ceramic wall hanging she'd made in the third grade, then presented to her aunt and uncle as a Christmas present. "I appreciate what you're trying to do, honest," she said, trying her best to be calm. "But what's happening between Jake and myself is just that—between Jake and myself. Jake got rid of the press today, and we don't need anything else to go wrong. We've both agreed to go slow and see what develops. And so far, even if you think we're boring, we're doing pretty darn well on our own. So no Donald, okay? *Promise* me, Aunt Bitzy."

Her aunt rolled her eyes. "Very well, Cookie, if you insist on being dull and plodding," she said in resignation. "But you didn't get your lack of dramatic flair from the Yardley side of the family, let me tell you. And you really should read a few of my favorite author's books. Araminta Raven would have used Donald for all he was worth!"

Jake put down the letter from one of his clients, a communication concerning royalty rights he had been reading without digesting for the past fifteen minutes, and walked out onto the patio behind his rented house.

It was nearly midnight, and he couldn't sleep. Nor could he concentrate on his work. He couldn't do much of anything, as a matter of fact, other than ask himself, over and over again, why he was alone in one house while Susannah was alone in another one, when everything that was in him was crying out that they should be together. Together tonight. Together tomorrow. Together for all the days and nights there might be.

Was he destined to always fall in love all at once, in little more than a heartbeat—and then pay for his impetuous commitments for the rest of his life?

Or had Jennifer been an aberration, and Susannah was the real thing? And how could he know? How could he take the chance of committing himself again when, this time, his heart would not be the only one broken if he was wrong?

For now he had Alex to consider as well as himself. Alex who, thanks to Belinda Yardley, already saw Susannah as a possible mother, a soft, feminine influence on his motherless childhood.

Susannah had come into both their lives when they were vulnerable, adapting to a new place, a new environment, a life-style far removed from the glitz and glitter of Manhattan.

She excited Jake even as she soothed him, caused him to indulge in daydreams populated by scenes of the three of them sitting in front of the fireplace in his new home, sharing a pew with Aunt Bitzy on Sundays before heading off to the local pancake house, taking walks in the twilight, Alex pushing the stroller containing his new baby sister or brother....

So different from the life he had led with Jennifer. So normal, so domestic—and yet with that constant undercurrent of passion that assailed his senses each time he looked at Susannah, each time his hand brushed against hers, each time he took her in his arms and kissed her, the single time he had made sweet, searing love with her....

Should he tell her the truth? *All* of the truth? If he hoped that anything could ever come from this attraction, this love—he was sure it must be love—they felt for each other, he would have to tell her the truth sooner or later.

Better sooner, he thought, unconsciously stripping the leaves from a low-hanging branch of the cherry tree beside the patio.

After all, her life was in Manhattan. Her business was in Manhattan. How would she react when he told her, if he told her, that he was in the process of selling his law practice in New York to become a general-practice lawyer here in Allentown?

He had hinted to her that he wanted to do some pro bono work in the area, but he hadn't told her how very much of his time he planned to devote to working with those who could not afford to pay for legal representation.

Yes, he still had his income from his parents' estate, and that was more than enough to keep up his life-style. By the first of the year he would have the proceeds of the sale of his law practice—no inconsiderable sum. Money wasn't a problem, had never been a problem.

Asking Susannah to give up her business in Manhattan, and the life of an independent city woman—

now *that* was a problem. He had already seen what even the thought of such a transformation from the big city to the small-town life had done to his marriage to Jennifer. When he had suggested a move to Connecticut after Alex was born, she had reacted by sleeping with his most prosperous client, then recounting the affair to Jake at that client's next dinner party.

Stop it! he warned himself silently, turning on his heel and going back into the house. *Stop comparing them. Susannah is not Jennifer. Susannah doesn't play games. She's too real, too honest, to ever play that sort of game....*

The countdown to Emily's demise was well under way by Tuesday morning, with Fred Gibbons stopping by to mark the tree trunk and larger branches with chalk precisely where he planned to make his first cuts. It was rather like watching the beginnings of an autopsy, and Susannah had quite lost her appetite for breakfast by the time she met Jake on his patio.

"You're just in time for some of Maria's one-of-a-kind waffles," Jake told her, holding out her chair for her, then nuzzling her nape when the housekeeper turned to go back into the kitchen. "Hmm, you taste delicious. Would you please pass the maple syrup? I think I'll skip the waffles and just nibble on you instead."

Fighting the shiver that skipped down her spine at his touch, Susannah replied, "I'm glad one of us is hungry, or else Maria might be insulted. I've just been to view the body and give my condolences to the chief mourners. They appear to be taking it pretty well, all things considered, although Aunt Bitzy seemed a little misty-eyed when Fred told her he'd have no trouble ripping apart the tree house and getting rid of all the 'junk.' I could really hate that man, you know, and I don't even know him.''

"He does seem to enjoy his work, doesn't he?'' Jake commented, taking up the chair across from hers, squinting in the bright sunlight as he looked across the lawn to where Emily stood, patiently waiting for the end. "If there were any other way—''

"Stop right there! Don't let Aunt Bitzy hear you talking like that,'' Susannah objected, waving a fork at him, "or she'll have you getting second opinions until Emily dies of old age.''

Jake winced in an exaggerated way, suddenly resembling his young son very much. "Well, at least we won't be bothered with any more reporters now that the story is dying a natural death. Although you might be flattered to know that the reporter who came here yesterday, Stephen Wadlow, told me he'd had a great response to the Princess in the Tree House article. I promised him we'd keep in touch if there were any new developments.''

"Oh, you did, did you?'' Susannah lowered her eyes, hoping to hide her reaction to his gentle teasing. "And do you think there might be any 'new developments'?''

Jake took a long sip of his coffee, his dark eyes suddenly turning solemn as he looked at her over the rim of the cup. "That depends. We still have almost a month before you go back to the city. Are you anxious to return?"

"Manhattan in the dog days of August? Hardly," Susannah told him honestly. "I'll take Robert the swing and Aunt Bitzy's shady back porch any day, thank you. But I do have to go back eventually. It's sort of difficult running a one-person business when that one person is living in another state."

Jake pushed himself closer to the table, resting his elbows on the white lace place mat. "So I've found," he said, his gaze now so intent Susannah fought the urge to wipe at her chin, sure she had dripped maple syrup there. "Which is why—" He hesitated, softly clearing his throat before continuing, "Why I've decided to sell my practice and open an office here in Allentown."

Susannah was silent for several moments, mostly because she couldn't come up with a single coherent thing to say. All she could think of was that she would soon be back in Manhattan, while Jake and Alex would be here, in Pennsylvania, over eighty miles away from her. He wouldn't even be coming into the city two days a week.

Absence makes the heart grow fonder, her brain told her, as clichés were very comforting at times.

Out of sight, out of mind, her absent aunt, the acknowledged expert in clichés, whispered to her emotions.

So much for taking it slow, allowing the relationship time to grow.

"How—how nice," Susannah commented at last, reaching for her own coffee cup, then deciding against taking a sip of coffee because she knew it couldn't possibly get past the lump in her throat. "Then you'll be giving up entertainment law?"

She listened, careful to keep smiling, and to insert the occasional "Uh-huh," and "Wonderful!" at the appropriate times, while Jake explained how he planned to divide his time between a general practice of law and pro bono work at a local law clinic.

Professor Allerson's desk, she thought, remembering how earnest Jake had been when he had spoken of his old teacher. I should have known. *I should have sensed then that he was trying to tell me something. The law professor hadn't only made an impression on his student, he had helped to shape his life, the man he had become. And, oh, how she loved the man he had become!*

When Jake stopped talking, his words seeming to trail off as he awaited her reaction to his news, she offered quietly, "Alex must be thrilled to know that he'll have his father home with him every night."

Jake nodded, smiling, and seemed suddenly more relaxed, as if he felt better after making his declaration. "He's already talking about volunteering me to help coach his soccer team. And, of course, we'll have to start doing some serious shopping for that minivan now."

"Won't you miss the excitement of New York? I mean, the shows, the museums, the nightlife?"

He shook his head. "In the words of my son, who got them heaven knows where—'Been there, done that.' No, Cookie, I won't miss any of it. Besides, Manhattan isn't on the other side of the moon. I already know I can be there in just under two hours."

"And you'll visit me from time to time?" she asked, pinning the brightest smile she could summon on her seemingly frozen face and trying not to wince at her obvious plea for his attention.

"Visit you?" His answering smile appeared similarly strained. "Of course. We can go to a show. I have connections to get us choice tickets, you understand."

So this is the kiss-off, Susannah thought, looking into the future and seeing herself sitting by the telephone, waiting for Jake's calls, calls that would become fewer and further apart. Oh, he might mean well, but long-distance relationships seldom worked.

As long as she had believed he would be coming into Manhattan twice a week she hadn't worried, had felt there was time for their relationship to grow on its own, time for Jake to bury the last of his past and declare himself ready to love again, to commit again. She would see him in Manhattan, she would visit him here in Allentown.

But now...now that had all changed. How often could she make the drive to Aunt Bitzy's before she looked pathetically eager for his company, before their relationship changed from growing to stagnant, before her aunt threw a copy of one of Araminta Raven's books at her and chirped, "I told you so!"

Susannah patted her mouth with her napkin and rose, saying, "Well, that was delicious," knowing that more than half the waffle still sat, cold and untouched, on her plate. "Shall we go see what our two tree-house-sitters are up to?"

Jake looked at her quizzically, as if he wanted to say something more to her, then fell into step beside her as they headed across the lawn, the subject of Jake's new Allentown-based career left behind them.

"Who's that?" Jake asked as they approached Emily.

Susannah, walking with her head down and caught up in her own thoughts, looked up to see a tall, slim blond man standing at the base of the elm tree, apparently holding a conversation with her aunt, who was sitting on the front porch of the tree house, Alex perched cross-legged beside her.

"I haven't a clue," Susannah lied, knowing without being told that she was looking at Matilda Mathewson's grandson, Donald the veterinarian. *Darn it!* she grumbled to herself. *When are you going to learn to check Aunt Bitzy for crossed fingers when she's making a promise?*

"I hope it isn't another reporter," she improvised swiftly, mentally thinking up hideous tortures to use on her meddling aunt. "Don't those guys ever give up?"

"Yoo-hoo! Cookie!" Aunt Bitzy trilled as Susannah and Jake approached. "Look who's here. It's Donald Mathewson. *Doctor* Donald Mathewson. You remember, don't you? He's come to invite you to dinner!" Then, as if she had just seen him, which Susannah knew she hadn't, her aunt added, "Oh, Jake. I didn't see you. Aren't you supposed to be in New York today? It is Tuesday, isn't it?"

I ought to donate all her romance novels to the local library and cancel her subscriptions to all her book clubs, Susannah thought in mingled anger and embarrassment.

And then she reconsidered her reaction. Why shouldn't she have dinner with Matilda Mathewson's grandson? There weren't any rings on her finger—or through her nose. Jake Longstreet didn't own her, didn't seem to want to own her.

For all his talk of letting their relationship grow slowly, for all his kisses, he had just about come out this morning and told her that, after she had finished decorating his new house, she was free to leave for Manhattan at any time. He and Alex, however, were living in Allentown now, and would be fully occupied in building their lives there, practicing law there, even coaching soccer there. They had no room for fairy-tale romance and happy endings interfering with that blossoming father-son bond.

"Get rid of him," Jake gritted out quietly from beside Susannah, startling her, and she looked up at him hopefully, wanting to see how he looked when he was jealous. But he didn't look jealous. He just looked impatient, as if Donald Mathewson had intruded in an area he had no business invading.

"Get rid of him?" Susannah repeated in a whisper. "What do you want me to do? Shoot him? He's standing on *your* precious property. *You* get rid of him!"

She shouldn't have challenged Jake. She should have poked him in the ribs, smiled, and said, "Geronimo!" Then they could have laughed, and talked to Donald the veterinarian for a few minutes, and then gone off to visit the shops she'd marked in the Yellow Pages and pick out wallpaper together. She could have stuck by his side like wallpaper paste, until he couldn't imagine life without her, until he asked her to become part of his world.

But Jake had just finished giving her one too many pieces of information, and one too many orders, and Susannah had felt her temper flare. Leaving Jake where he stood, she walked up to Donald, her right hand extended, and said in a loud, clear voice, "Donald! How lovely to meet you at last. I've heard so much about you from my aunt. Dinner? I'd love to!"

"Hey, Dad, where'ya going?" Alex called out, giving Susannah her only clue that Jake had returned to his rented house, for she certainly wasn't going to turn around and watch as he walked out of her life.

12

---·◄—

Dinner with Dr. Donald Mathewson lasted longer than the Hundred Years War, her three and one half years in teeth braces, and the age of disco all wrapped up into one.

Not that Donald wasn't a nice man. He was nice. He was very nice. He just wasn't Jake Longstreet. Nobody was like Jake Longstreet. Not even Jake Longstreet.

Susannah had thought she was beginning to know the man, understand him. But she had been wrong.

She had thought he was honest, but he couldn't be honest with her, not when he had yet to learn to be honest with himself.

She had thought he loved her, but he couldn't be in love with her, not when he still had not learned to trust another woman not to do to him what Jennifer Merchant had so cruelly, effectively done.

She had thought they might have a future together, but they wouldn't, at least not until he could stop hiding behind his past and take a step into that future.

And not, she reminded herself as she headed for Emily, flashlight in hand, until she, too, was completely honest, admitting to herself, and to him, that going slow, playing it safe, was absolutely the worst idea in the history of the world.

Conflict. Susannah shivered at the thought of the word. Her Aunt Bitzy could take conflict, and Araminta Raven, and Donald the veterinarian from Virginia, stuff them all in a hat, and then toss it in the nearest garbage can. Love didn't need conflict. Love needed communication, and trust, and honesty.

Jake didn't want to let her go. Susannah knew that now, after spending an evening smiling politely at Donald's tales of his animal patients and mentally kicking herself as she thought over the events of the day.

Jake hadn't been letting her down easy. Where had she gotten such a cockamamy idea, anyway? He had been feeling her out, telling her about his decision to set up his practice solely in Allentown, and then watching for her reaction—trying to gauge without asking whether she would be willing to give up her life in New York, her career in the big city, for the life of a lawyer's wife.

Why hadn't she seen that immediately? Had she really been so unsure of their relationship that she was seeing bogeyman where none existed? Yeah. That was possible. More than possible. It had happened.

What a jerk she was! A card-carrying idiot!

And then, just to top things off, she had used poor Donald to get back at Jake—just like some high school freshman playing silly games.

Stupid. Stupid. Stupid!

You made love with the man, she reminded herself as she climbed the curving steps to the porch of the tree house. *You made love with the man, but you couldn't find the words to tell him you're in love with him? To tell him that you don't want to go slow, you don't want to be safe. How do you allow a man the intimacy of your body and deny him the intimacy of your mind, your heart?*

She balanced the flashlight on the edge of the small table, aimed in the direction of the cupboard, and knelt down to retrieve her china collection, packing the small cups and saucers in newspaper before carefully placing each piece in the shoe box she had brought with her.

Slowly, and not without shedding a few tears, she then gathered up the remainder of her childhood treasures, stowing them in the green plastic trash bag she had tucked into her pocket before leaving the kitchen and walking through the darkness for one last, solitary visit with Emily.

"Cookie?"

Susannah quickly wiped at her tears with the hem of her shirt before opening the door to the tree house porch and watching as her aunt levered herself into the rocking chair that sat perilously close to the edge. "Aunt Bitzy? Why aren't you in bed?"

"I couldn't sleep," the woman answered, beginning to rock. "And as the stars always seem brighter from up here, I thought I'd visit awhile with Emily. Are you all packed up?"

"Uh-hmm," Susannah answered, putting the bag to one side and sitting down on the porch, allowing her long legs to hang over the side. "From now on, I suppose my memories will be the portable kind. How do you think the rag rug will look in my apartment?"

"Not having seen your apartment, I wouldn't know. So you still plan to leave when Jake's house is done? I had thought—"

"Thought he'd track me down at the restaurant, bust poor, innocent Donald one in the chops, and then carry me off to the nearest preacher?" Susannah volunteered, beginning to swing her legs back and forth in the way she had as a child. She looked over her shoulder at her aunt. "Or are you here to suggest Plan B?"

"Don't be sarcastic, young lady," Aunt Bitzy warned, "as it doesn't suit you. I made a mistake. I admit it. But, after what you told me this afternoon—all this business about Jake giving up his practice in Manhattan—I think I have recognized the plot flaw."

"Back to Romance Writing 101, are we?" Susannah rolled her eyes. "Oh, goody."

"I'm going to ignore that outburst as well, Cookie, as I know you're feeling particularly mulish at the moment. However—"

"Why is there always a 'however'?" Susannah asked, a smile tugging, unbidden, at the corners of her mouth. "Okay, Aunt Bitzy—shoot!"

"I found a book I had purchased on the art of writing and in it I discovered a chapter on sagging middles. That's what we're dealing with here, you know. You have stumbled into a sagging middle."

"Great. Now I need a literary girdle!" Susannah exploded, beginning to laugh.

"We are speaking of the figurative, Cookie, not the literal," the former teacher explained calmly, as if speaking to a sweet, but faintly thick student. "And the reason for that sagging middle—the reason you can't get from here to there—is that you and Jake are suffering from a lack of communication. That makes for a bad, *bad,* book. In other words, if you and Jake were just to sit down for five minutes, and *talk* to each other, everything would be fine. And so I told him tonight."

Susannah, who had been mentally conjuring up a picture of a book with a potbelly bulge at its center, stopped smiling at her aunt's last words. "You did *what!* Oh, Aunt Bitzy—how could you?"

The ever-literal woman replied calmly, "Well, I think that should be simple to understand. I walked across the yards and knocked on his door. It wasn't the easiest thing I've ever done, but Jake was very good about listening to me. He's sorry he misbehaved this afternoon, by the way."

"Misbehaved? Is that your word or his?"

"Mine, Cookie. He said he'd acted like a total ass, but I don't like to repeat things that might make someone appear in a bad light. Anyway, he said that—just for a moment—he saw you using another man to make him jealous, which is precisely what Alex's mother used to do, the shameless hussy, Lord rest her soul. But now that I've explained that I nearly forced you into going to dinner with Donald, he has forgiven you. Isn't that nice?"

The air temperature, Susannah had heard on the radio not a half hour ago, was seventy-nine degrees. Her body temperature, now that her aunt had explained that Jake had "forgiven" her, was nearing Death Valley record highs. "He *forgave* me?" she questioned. "Quick, call the Nobel committee. I think Jake gets the humanitarian award this year."

"This isn't going well, is it?" Aunt Bitzy asked, her tone rather sheepish. "Now do you see what I mean? If the two of you were only to sit down and talk to each other—with you explaining that you'd love nothing better than to live in Allentown, and with him explaining that he was only afraid you'd be forced to give up your career in New York if he were to ask you to stay here with him—why, then everything would be settled. Why do you insist on making things so difficult, Cookie?"

"*I'm* making things difficult?" Susannah all but shouted, silencing the crickets that had been chirping in the long grass at the base of the tree. "I'm making things difficult?" she repeated, looking around her for something she could throw, or smash, or grind into bits between her teeth. "I come to Allentown to rescue my sweet old aunt from a tree, get my rear end plastered all over the local papers, fall in love with an idiot who can't figure out that I'm not his dead wife—and *I'm* being difficult? I try to do a good deed and the next thing I know I'm part of a romance novel—the sagging middle part, no less. And now everything is *my* fault? Oh, that does it," she said, picking up the trash bag and heading for the steps. "That just *does* it!"

"Cookie? Where are you going?"

"Where am I going?" Susannah gritted out from between clenched teeth. "I'll tell you where I'm going, Aunt Bitzy. I'm going to bed. And then, in the morning, I'm going home. To New York. To where—and I can't believe I'm saying this—all the *sane* people live!"

She didn't leave, of course. How could she leave, with so much left unsaid, undone?

But that didn't mean she was ready to see Jake that Wednesday morning, although she did watch from behind Emily's thick trunk as he escorted Alex, weighted down by his sleeping bag and a small canvas knapsack, to the camp bus.

Let him stew for a few hours, she told herself as she employed Uncle Frank's handy-dandy winch to lower the rocking chair safely to the ground, then lugged the thing back to Aunt Bitzy's front porch.

And I'm not playing games, either, she repeated quietly for at least the tenth time as she indulged herself in an hour-long bubble bath followed by a pedicure, a manicure, and another quiet hour spent stretched out on her bed, damp tea bags on eyelids that were still suspiciously swollen from the bout of tears she had succumbed to the previous night.

I'm simply being adult about things, she convinced herself as, for lack of anything else to do, she picked up one of Araminta Raven's books and childishly headed for the front porch, where she was confident Jake couldn't see her.

Three hours later, with tears in her eyes and a dreamy expression on her face, Susannah closed the book, rubbing the back cover in satisfaction at the story of love triumphant.

Pity there aren't any pirates in Allentown, she found herself thinking before she could bring herself up short, realizing that she was beginning to think like Aunt Bitzy, which couldn't be considered a good thing—could it?

"What are you doing, Aunt Bitzy?" she asked curiously as she followed her nose, which led her directly to the kitchen and the source of the lovely smell of warm chocolate-chip cookies. "Didn't you just bake a batch the other day?"

"I bake a batch every day, Cookie, which you'd know if you paid attention," her aunt answered evenly, sliding another tray of spoon-size dough drops into the wall oven. "Two double batches, actually. Glynis and I have gone into business."

Susannah frowned. "Glynis?"

"Yes, Glynis. From the pancake house, and quite my most brilliant student when it came to finding customers for our school's annual magazine-sales drive. She was top salesperson two years in row, partly because I felt I had to hold her back a year—she didn't mature quite as rapidly as most seven-year-olds, you understand," her aunt explained as she sat on her favorite kitchen chair, the one with the red-and-white-checked padded seat.

"I hated sharing my secret recipe," she continued, "but now that the orders have become so large, Glynis is preparing two double batches a day as well, so that we can keep up with the orders. I'm going to talk to Jake about incorporating soon, as I think Aunt Bitzy's Cookies is about to become big business. Glynis phoned just this morning to say that a supermarket chain has called, and is *extremely* interested in my cookies."

"Where have I been?" Susannah asked the ceiling, which is where she turned when looking at her innocently smiling aunt proved more upsetting than she would have considered possible. "I have been living in this house, haven't I? So why didn't I see what was going on? Alex couldn't have been eating all those cookies. Even I, in my heyday as a chocolate chip freak, couldn't have eaten all those cookies. Lord, I must be the world's biggest jerk!"

"You've been otherwise occupied," Aunt Bitzy told her kindly. "What with falling in love, and making mistake after mistake—"

"Thanks, doll," Susannah groused good-humoredly, slowly subsiding into the closest chair. "That helps a lot." She leaned her elbows on the tabletop and peered at her aunt. "So, the supermarket chain to one side, where are you peddling your cookies? And why haven't I seen you and a fully-packed Rachel running around town, making your deliveries?"

"Glynis does the actual legwork, if I have that term correctly," Aunt Bitzy explained, pulling open the drawer beneath the ancient kitchen table. She extracted about a dozen brown paper bags with the words "Aunt Bitzy's Cookies" stamped on one side in bright red ink, and began filling them, six saucer-size cookies to a bag.

"Right now," she continued, "we're selling them in local grocery stores and even a few gasoline stations, so it's not too difficult to make deliveries. But I see big things for Aunt Bitzy's Cookies. Really I do, which is fortunate, as you don't seem to be giving me any reason to spend a quiet old age hoping for a few grandnieces and -nephews to rock in Robert."

"Slip in that needle any time you can, don't you, Aunt Bitzy?" Susannah asked rhetorically, as the first rumbles of thunder could be heard in the distance, warning of the storms that were predicted to arrive later that evening. "Well, don't go global too soon.

That lovely lap of yours might be needed sooner than you think, because I've decided to take a page from Araminta Raven's latest book and *talk* to the man. Should I just wander over to Jake's house sometime after dinner, or do you think I should crawl there on my hands and knees?''

Aunt Bitzy manned the stapler, neatly sealing each brown bag. ''Why ask me, Cookie? I'm sure I have absolutely no opinion in the matter.''

Susannah quipped, ''Well, that would be a first!'' as she swiped a warm cookie from the pile still to be packed and made her exit to her bedroom.

Jake let go of the drape, so that it swung down and across the rain-wet window once more, blocking out the sight of Belinda Yardley's brightly glowing kitchen window. ''That's the last damned time I'll take advice on my love life from a woman who quotes from romance novels!'' he exclaimed as he turned to face the room once more, then smiled sheepishly as he saw Maria standing in the doorway, dressed for her evening out. ''Sorry about that, Maria,'' he said, clearing his throat. ''I guess I was talking to myself.''

''And now you're talking to me,'' the housekeeper said flatly as she plucked an umbrella from the wrought-iron stand beside the front door. ''Keep going, Mr. Jake, and you'll find the right one yet. She's tall, blond, and has legs meant more for looking at than marching with, but she'll do. She'll do—and it's about time Alex had a mother, if you ask me.''

"Which I didn't," Jake reminded the retired servicewoman with a smile. "But if you're giving me an order, I promise to follow it to the letter."

"Then I'll leave you to it, sir. Ah, what a night for a sleep-over. It reminds me of maneuvers in South Carolina. Rained the whole week. Of course, Alex and his crew are in cabins, not tents, so they'll just pass the time listening to the thunder and telling ghost stories," Maria ended as she opened the door on the dark, rainy sky, saluted in a decidedly unmilitary way, and headed off to see the double feature with the widower who lived on the other side of Jake's new house.

His mind made up—either by him or for him, he wasn't sure—Jake headed for the laundry room and the dark green rain slicker he'd seen there earlier in the day. It wouldn't exactly be romantic, showing up on Susannah's back porch, dripping wet and "rubberized," but he wasn't going to allow this breach between them to continue for another day.

He was going to tell her the truth—all of the truth, including the parts that made him look like a thickheaded, jealous, unforgiving idiot—and then ask her to stick around, to give them both the time they needed to build the base that would serve as the foundation, he hoped, for the life they would have together.

And if she looked at him with even a quarter of the emotion she showed when she looked at Alex, he might just tell her he was in love with her, and the hell with being careful!

So thinking, and with the hood of the slicker pulled close around his bent head, he swung open the door to the patio, took two steps onto the bricks and into the pouring rain—and nearly knocked down the woman he was on his way to see.

"Jake! I—" Susannah, looking like a drenched daffodil in her yellow slicker, exclaimed as he grabbed her arms to steady her, a streak of lightning turning the patio into a brief puddle of light.

"Susannah! I was just on my way to—"

"I couldn't care less about Donald Mathewson!" she shouted above a clap of thunder.

"You're *not* Jennifer!" Jake yelled as the wind whipped rain across his face, blowing the hood off his head so that he was instantly drenched. "You never were Jennifer. Susannah—I'm such an *ass!*"

"No—no, it was *me*. I sent all the wrong signals—"

"I took advantage of you that night—"

"You took nothing I wasn't willing to give—"

"We moved too fast—"

"And then there was Emily, and the reporters, and the house—"

"And Alex, and the pancake house, and Aunt Bitzy's romance novels—"

"But now that Emily comes down tomorrow—"

"And we can spend all our time decorating the house...my house...some day...one day...maybe even our—"

"Jake!" Susannah shouted as lightning ripped through the sky once more, followed closely by a boom of thunder that shook the windowpanes behind them. "I'm drowning!"

Laughing, and feeling as young and vital as some god of the storm, Jake pulled Susannah into his arms and kissed her, holding her close as the storm swirled around them, feeling whole and cleansed by both the rain and her touch—and their abruptly blurted honesty.

"Geronimo," he whispered after breaking the kiss, his mouth close beside her ear as he pulled her with him, back into the house. "Not that I'm trying to call a halt, you understand," he said as he divested himself of the slicker, then helped Susannah hang hers on the hook beside his. "I just thought a change of venue was in order. Do you think I can make coffee without letting you go?"

"You'd need a court order to get rid of me, Counselor," she answered, moving into his arms once more, so that he forgot that they were both wet, and shivering, and probably asking for twin cases of double pneumonia.

He wanted this woman, wanted her and needed her and loved her with an intensity that frightened him. Aunt Bitzy had said the two of them needed nothing more than to sit and talk to each other for a few minutes and they'd both understand how perfectly they had been made for each other.

Yeah, well, talking was always good. Maybe he'd even write her a letter—but not now. Now, all Jake could do was hold Susannah, kiss her, press her long, slim body against his, and leave the words for later. Besides, some small imp of mischief whispered into his ear, *Actions speak louder than words.*

And telephones rang louder than thunder.

"We'll ignore it," Jake grumbled against Susannah's lips as his hands worked at the buttons of her blouse.

"Uh-hmm," she answered as they stumbled, together, toward the darkened living room, and the couch that beckoned to them, promising a private haven away from the storm, and the world, for as long as they both desired.

"Damn it!" Jake exploded when the phone stopped ringing, only to begin its annoying peal again a few moments later.

Susannah stretched out on the couch, her long blond hair, damp with rain, spread out like a halo around her. "You'd better answer it, Jake. Then take it off the hook."

Taking a deep breath, which did little to calm him, Jake picked up the receiver and barked an annoyed "Hello!" into it, which was the last thing he said for a full minute, as his blood ran colder than the evening rain, and his heart began pounding in fear.

"What do you mean, Alex isn't there?" he yelled into the receiver at last, causing Susannah to bolt to an upright position and begin rebuttoning her blouse. "How the hell do you lose a nine-year-old kid?"

"Oh my God," Susannah breathed quietly, coming to stand close beside Jake, her hand squeezing his shoulder. "Alex is missing? In this storm?"

Jake was listening again, his hand pressed hard against his mouth. "Yes, yes," he said a moment later, nodding just as if the camp counselor could see him. "I know who Emily is. I'll call you back!"

He hung up and began running toward the back door. "Alex disappeared over two hours ago," he told Susannah as she raced after him. "They've been searching the campgrounds, but then one of the kids told them Alex bragged that he wasn't sleeping in any stupid cabin. He was going to sleep with Emily, and have a *real* adventure."

Susannah pushed her arms into the still-dripping slicker, running a hand through her wet hair. "Why didn't they call you sooner?"

"Because they didn't believe the kid, that's why," Jake explained, trying to find the sleeve of the green slicker, then throwing the thing to the floor in disgust. "Why would a nine-year-old be going off to sleep with someone named Emily? Not only that, Cookie, but the counselor told me they checked—Alex called a taxi to bring him home." He opened the back door, which immediately blew against the side of the house in the strong wind. "My God—a taxi! Does he think he's still in Manhattan?"

Susannah grabbed his arm, making him walk when he wanted to run, employing the flashlight she had brought with her to guide their way across the wide sweep of lawn and toward the tree house. "It's Emily's last night, Jake," she said, her voice raised against the nearly constant rumble of thunder. "Alex wanted to camp out in the tree house, like I did when I was a kid. Lord, there's nothing there anymore. I waited until he left for camp before I took everything away, but Alex is sitting in an empty tree house. No rug, no quilt in the corner— Oh, *Jake!*"

"He's probably scared out of his mind, which serves him right," Jake said, trying to sound stern, when he was silently praying that Alex was snug and dry somewhere—anywhere but in the storm-damaged tree that had been judged and found unsafe in times like these.

He felt disoriented, the flashing lightning, the claps of thunder, the slashing rain and the blowing leaves all combining to alter the familiar landscape around them, causing shadows to dance like childhood visions of large-toothed monsters that only come out on dark, stormy nights.

I should have let Fred cut it down that first day, Jake told himself as he stopped a moment to help Susannah, who had stumbled over the edge of a small rock garden at the rear of his rented property. Still holding hands, they entered the stand of trees that separated Jake's property from Belinda Yardley's. *I should have acted like a parent, and not like some pitiful man trying to be a friend to his son.*

"We're here!" Susannah exclaimed, reaching out a hand to touch the railing of Uncle Frank's sturdy winding steps. "Alex!" she shouted, giving the railing a shake. *"Alex!"*

Jake pushed past her, not caring that he could advance only by feel and not by sight, not thinking of anything but finding his son, and holding him close....

"Daddy!" Alex cried, opening the door to the tree house just as Jake collapsed onto the porch, his vision clouded by the rain in his face, the tears in his eyes. "Daddy—I'm so scared! Emily's *groaning!*"

Jake gathered his son into his arms, leaving behind Alex's knapsack, and the two of them picked their way down the steps, back to the relative safety of the ground.

"Let's get away from these trees!" Jake shouted to Susannah, who was hugging a sobbing Alex. "Emily is groaning."

Susannah looked at him quizzically, but didn't ask any questions. Each of them holding one of Alex's hands, they headed back to the house in as close to a dead run as possible just as, behind them, a white-hot streak of lightning slammed into the small stand of trees.

Epilogue

> ◆━━━◆

Cupid Employs Lightning Bolt In Shot To The Heart
Reported by Stephen Wadlow

The saga of Emily the elm tree ended with a bang rather than a whimper two days ago when lightning struck, exploding the tree house and reducing Emily to kindling. Belinda Yardley, who had been protesting the removal of the tree by maintaining a vigil on the front porch of the decades-old tree house nestled in its branches, reported that no one was injured when the tree was struck during the height of the storm.

However, this reporter has learned, Emily's demise did not come before the Princess of the Tree House was saved from disaster during a last-minute rescue by her true love, proving once more that there are still happy endings in this age of almost unremitting bad news.

So, Alex, when's the wedding?

"At least it's a good picture of Alex," Susannah supplied weakly as she looked over Jake's shoulder at the photograph of Alex as he stood in front of Emily, the proud old elm now split nearly in half, the ground around the trunk littered with the remnants of the tree house.

Jake folded the newspaper and tossed it onto the brick patio, then shook his head. "I'm surprised the guy dared to put his byline on the story. He's yet to get his facts right. All that crap about Cupid, and weddings! And it sounds as if I rescued *you* from Emily, not Alex."

"Aunt Bitzy told the reporter that last part," Susannah informed him, moving to sit in the chair facing Jake's. "She thought it might not be good for Alex if word leaked out that he had run away from camp and nearly gotten himself fried when that lightning hit. Something about being labeled as a wild kid in school, or something like that, which we all know isn't true at all. Alex is an angel. He just wanted to say a last farewell to Emily. What's really the matter, Jake? Don't you like being written up as some sort of superhero Prince Charming?"

"An *anonymous* Prince Charming," he added, as Stephen Wadlow had once more failed to mention his name in his article.

"Again, Aunt Bitzy's idea. She warned Mr. Wadlow last week that he was not to use your name, just in case one of the wire services picked up the story. And he agreed. So much for *all* reporters being bloodsucking leeches, huh?"

"Well, I'll be damned!" Jake stood, holding out a hand to help Susannah to rise, then walked with her toward his new house. "I think I've just encountered another perk connected to living in Allentown. Small-town heart lives, I guess, even in a city this size." He turned to smile at her. "The workmen have quit for the day. Want to see if two people actually can fit in that new bathtub?"

Susannah tipped her head to one side, as if considering his invitation. "I don't know, Jake. Aunt Bitzy and Alex are helping Glynis deliver today's quota of cookies, so I guess no one would miss me. But do princesses cavort in bathtubs? I wouldn't want to ruin my image. Besides, I thought that, leaving that reporter's romantic nonsense to one side, we'd agreed to take things slow for a while."

Jake turned to her, drawing her into his arms. "And a sterling idea that was—until the lightning struck," he said seriously, nuzzling the soft, sun-kissed skin of her throat. "I'm not real big on signs and portents, but a lightning bolt is pretty hard to ignore."

"Really. And?"

"And I think it's time you agreed to marry me, Susannah Yardley. Neither of us has exactly said the words, but we are in love, aren't we? I know I am.

Anyway, I figure I'll plant Emily II as soon as Fred disposes of the remains of her predecessor, so that we can exchange our vows right here, in our new backyard. And I plan to pay particular attention to the until-death-do-you-part business, because I want this to be forever."

"Go on, I'm listening," Susannah said quietly, stroking his cheek with the back of her hand.

"You can start decorating the house now if you want to, but the bulk of it can wait until we're back from our honeymoon. I'm sure Aunt Bitzy will agree to watch Alex while I take you to Paris. I've never been there, but I'm sure we'll both love it, and we'd be back before the new school term, and..."

His voice trailed away as he grinned sheepishly, realizing he was doing it again, making plans without any thought that she would protest. "Cookie?" he ventured, looking at her as if for help.

Susannah melted against him, gazing up into his flashing blue eyes. "If you're waiting for me to yell Geronimo, darling," she said, slipping her hand around his neck in order to pull his head down toward hers, "I'm afraid you're in for a very long wait."

* * * * *

Sneak Previews of December titles, from *Yours Truly*™:

CHRISTMAS KISSES FOR A DOLLAR
by Laurie Paige

Anne's selling kiss after chaste kiss at the Christmas fair—until a handsome rancher kisses her like they're under their own private mistletoe. By kiss number twenty, Anne's in love—with a man she can't ever marry!

HOLIDAY HUSBAND
by Hayley Gardner

Single Scrooge Sharon Fontaine challenges an anonymous Santa to find her the man of her dreams for Christmas. And on December 25th, a tall, dark and gorgeous gift, wrapped in a red ribbon, is waiting under her tree....

Available this month, from *Yours Truly*™:

SINGLE FEMALE (RELUCTANTLY) SEEKS...
by Dixie Browning

HUSBANDS DON'T GROW ON TREES
by Kasey Michaels

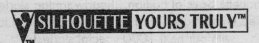

It's our 1000th Special Edition
and we're celebrating!

Join us these coming months for some wonderful
stories in a special celebration of our 1000th book
with some of your favorite authors!

Diana Palmer   **Nora Roberts**
Debbie Macomber   **Christine Flynn**
Phyllis Halldorson   **Lisa Jackson**

Plus miniseries by:

Lindsay McKenna, Marie Ferrarella, Sherryl Woods
and Gina Ferris Wilkins.

And many more books by special writers!

And as a special bonus, all Silhouette Special Edition
titles published during Celebration 1000! will have
**double** Pages & Privileges proofs of purchase!

Silhouette Special Edition...heartwarming stories
packed with emotion, just for you! You'll fall in love
with our next 1000 special stories!

WESTERN *Lovers*

Available in November

Two more
Western Lovers
ready to rope and tie your heart!

DESTINY'S CHILD—Ann Major
Once a Cowboy...
Texas cowboy Jeb Jackson laid claim to the
neighboring MacKay ranch, but feisty redhead
Megan MacKay refused to give up her land without
a fight. Surely Jeb could convince the headstrong
woman to come to an agreement—*and* become his
lovely bride!

YESTERDAY'S LIES—Lisa Jackson
Reunited Hearts
Years ago, Trask McFadden had wooed
Tory Wilson—only to put her father behind bars.
Now Trask was back, and Tory vowed she'd never
let him break her heart again—even if that meant
denying the only love she'd ever known....

WL1195